Dorran's father is supposed to be dead.

But he's not.

Dorran is finally settling in—things with Eli's parents are going well, even though Eli's mom is still uncomfortable with their relationship, and Eli seems to be more accepting of Dorran's ability to see ghosts and Francis' presence in their life.

Then Dorran opens his door to find his father, Angus, on the other side.

Dorran grew up thinking his father was dead. That's what his mother told him, and Dorran never doubted her. He clearly should have, though, and now he's confused and unsure whether or not he wants a relationship with his father.

But when Angus is arrested for the murder of his mother-in-law, Dorran can't abandon him. Angus might have done exactly that when Dorran was three, but that's not the kind of man Dorran is.

Alignment
Copyright © 2019 Catherine Lievens
ISBN: 978-1-4874-2756-6
Cover art by Angela Waters

Published by eXtasy Books Inc or
Devine Destinies, an imprint of eXtasy Books Inc

Look for us online at:
www.eXtasybooks.com or www.devinedestinies.com

Alignment
Lost in Translation Book 4

By

Catherine Lievens

DEDICATION

Alignment: in translation, the task of defining correspondences between source and translated texts.

CHAPTER ONE

Dorran knew what would happen the second he noticed Francis. He knew Francis well enough by now to understand. He just hoped Charlie wouldn't freak out as much as Eli had in the beginning and still did sometimes. Charlie wasn't like Eli, though. He didn't find what Dorran could do horrifying. He didn't want him to stop — which was good, because Dorran couldn't stop. He wished he could most of the time, but that wasn't happening. Carole had been clear. Dorran was never getting rid of his gift, and he needed to deal with that. That was why he was working with her to learn control, but it wasn't something Eli seemed to understand.

Charlie was different, though. He was Dorran's best friend, and he had been for years. More importantly, he thought that Dorran's ability to see ghosts was fun.

Dorran wouldn't say it was. He had to admit he enjoyed being able to see Francis and talk to him.

"May I?" Francis asked. He always asked when he wanted to use Dorran's energy to appear to people who didn't have Dorran's gift. He'd done it without asking a few times in the beginning, but he and Dorran had talked, and they'd come to an agreement.

Dorran didn't like being used, but this was Francis. He was part of Dorran's family, even though he was dead.

Dorran kept his focus on Charlie, who was talking about Theresa and their upcoming wedding. He hadn't noticed anything odd yet. Francis was still invisible to him, but he wouldn't be for long if he took Dorran's energy to appear.

Dorran nodded at Francis. Francis beamed, and Dorran rolled his eyes. Sometimes, he wondered what Francis would have done if Dorran hadn't had this gift. He loved talking to people, which usually meant Dorran, but now that Dorran knew what he could do and had a better grasp on how to do it, Francis could talk to more people. He didn't have a large group of friends, since Eli was wary of Dorran's gift and tended to ignore it rather than using it, but Carole visited often, and it looked like Charlie was about to be introduced to Francis officially.

"You're distracted. I understand wedding stuff isn't that interesting to you, but maybe you should start thinking about it," Charlie said.

Dorran blinked at him. "Start thinking about what?"

"You know, weddings."

"I got that the first time you said it, but I don't understand why I should."

Charlie poked Dorran's thigh with his socked foot. "Are you and Eli doing okay?"

Dorran scrunched his nose. "Yeah, but we're not ready to think about weddings, that's for sure."

"No? You won't try to beat Theresa and me to the altar?"

Dorran grabbed one of the pillows from the couch and hugged it to his chest. "We're not even living together yet."

"I thought you guys were waiting until after the wedding."

"Why do you think Eli and I are going to get married? I'm sure he never mentioned anything like that to you."

Charlie shrugged. "I don't know. I mean, you and Eli have a history together. You've known each other for what, twenty years?"

"Less than that."

"You know what I mean."

"I do, but it's not like we were together for all those years. We broke up when we were eighteen, remember? And we didn't see each other again until recently. We're not the same people we were at eighteen, and even if we were, I'm nowhere near ready for marriage."

But Dorran couldn't deny the idea sparked something in him. Would he and Eli ever get married? He didn't want what he and Eli had to disappear, but he wasn't sure. They'd had their problems, especially lately. They were working through them, and things were better now, but still. Dorran knew Eli wasn't happy about his gift and that he was still having a hard time accepting it. He knew that Eli's family didn't like them being together, even though they hadn't said anything to Dorran's face.

But they were trying, both Eli and his parents. So Dorran and Eli might not be ready for marriage, but they were ready for something more than what they'd had up until now. Dorran was still cautious, but he was hopeful.

"Holy shit!" Charlie yelled. He climbed onto the couch with both feet and pressed himself against the back of it.

Dorran chuckled and winked at Francis, who was sitting in his favorite armchair. "I thought I'd mentioned it. Charlie, this is Francis."

"And that's how you say it? Are you serious? He's dead."

"You already knew that. I'm not sure why you're surprised."

Charlie slowly slid down the couch, his hand pressed over his heart. "I guess I'm not. I just didn't expect him to appear like that. I thought we were alone."

Dorran chuckled. "Never think that. Francis has a habit of haunting his apartment. Again, you already knew that."

"I guess I was just surprised." Charlie cleared his throat. "What do I do now?"

Dorran rolled his eyes. "Francis, please put him out of his misery."

Francis raised a hand and wiggled his fingers at Charlie.

"Hi there. I'm Francis."

Dorran felt Charlie relax, even though he was still pressed against Dorran's side. "Hello, I guess."

"You guess?"

"Look, it's the first time I've talked to a ghost. I didn't even know I could." His eyes widened. "I have the same gift as you?" he asked, turning to look at Dorran.

Dorran shook his head. "No. Francis is using my energy to make himself visible to you. You wouldn't be able to see him otherwise."

Charlie's eyes stayed wide. "You mean like a leech?"

"Who are you calling a leech?" Francis asked.

"Shit. I didn't mean to offend you. I'm sorry."

Watching Charlie and Francis interact was fun. Eli tended to ignore Francis, and Francis didn't often make himself visible to him. He didn't want to. He tolerated Eli because he was Dorran's boyfriend, but he wasn't crazy about him, and until Eli finally came to terms with Dorran's ability and the fact that it wasn't going anywhere—and neither was Francis—things would stay tense between them. Dorran didn't like it, but there was nothing he could do about it, and he couldn't deny Eli had come a long way already. Hopefully, that would continue. Dorran wanted Eli in his life. He loved him. If he could choose, he'd choose Eli over his gift, but he couldn't. His gift was here to stay, and hopefully, so was Eli.

Francis laughed. "It's all right. I understand my existence is . . . peculiar."

Charlie snorted. "That's one way to say it." He eyed Dorran. "So this is what you deal with every day?"

"Pretty much. I mean, I see Francis most of the time, unless he doesn't want me to see him."

"That's usually when his boyfriend is here," Francis offered.

Charlie took a sip of his beer. "All right. Eli doesn't like you."

"That's one way to say it. I doubt Eli likes much of anything. He has a stick up his ass."

Charlie guffawed. "Yeah, Dorran's stick."

Dorran groaned. He'd expected something like this to happen. Charlie was a friendly guy, and he tended to take everything in stride. He'd been surprised when Francis had appeared, but he was already over that and making friends with Francis.

Dorran was glad. Francis needed more people than just him and Carole, especially since Carole didn't come around often. He'd never said anything, but he had to be lonely. It was a good thing Dorran worked from home, but he had to focus, and he couldn't spend his days talking to Francis. And when Eli was there, well. Francis usually disappeared. Dorran didn't know where, and sometimes, he suspected Francis was still around, just invisible. He certainly was always there when Dorran needed him for support or comfort.

And probably to spy on him and Eli when they had sex.

Dorran was uncomfortable with that idea, but he'd accepted the fact that he couldn't control Francis. As long as Francis didn't tell him what he saw and didn't reveal himself while they were going at it, Dorran was going to ignore it.

He leaned back against the couch and watched as Charlie and Francis talked about Dorran and Eli, then shifted to other topics. Dorran's life was weird, and nothing he would have imagined. He hadn't thought he'd see Eli again after they'd broken up, and he certainly hadn't thought he had the ability to see ghosts. Yet here he was, his best human friend and his best ghost friend talking as if it were perfectly normal.

And maybe it was, in Dorran's world. His life might not be conventional, but it certainly was never dull, and he was happy. He had friends and a boyfriend. He had a family, even though it was far from perfect. He had a job he enjoyed.

Everything was good.

Dorran wasn't sure whether Eli would come over or not this evening. They tried to spend as much time as they could together every day, and to at least text, but Eli's job was demanding. He had no way to know when he'd be assigned a new case, and most days, whether or not he'd be home for dinner. The fact that he still had his own apartment and a cat made everything more complicated, because he had to go there at least once a day. That meant he didn't come over as often as Dorran wished he could, and most of the time, they didn't spend a lot of time together.

Which was okay. Dorran wanted to spend more time with Eli, but this was life, and they needed to deal with it. He'd known what he was getting into when he'd agreed to date a cop. Besides, Dorran didn't mind spending time alone. He never was entirely alone, since Francis was around. Still, he missed Eli, and he couldn't help but smile when he heard the sound of a key in the lock of the front door.

Francis had been lounging in his armchair, and his head snapped toward the door when he heard it. He grimaced, then disappeared.

Dorran sighed. He wanted Francis and Eli to get along, but he knew it would take time. Besides, he had to admit he wanted some alone time with Eli. They didn't have nearly enough of it.

Dorran cleaned his hands and got to the door just as it opened, and Eli came in. He looked tired, but then he always did. Being a detective was Eli's dream job, but it didn't mean it wasn't hard on him.

Dorran smiled softly and reached for Eli. Eli dumped his messenger bag and wrapped his arms around Dorran, pulling him close.

They stood there, wrapped around each other, for several

moments. Dorran could feel Eli relaxing against him, the tension of the day draining from him. He was glad to be able to give that to Eli. He wished he had more to offer when it came to this, but it was better than nothing. If he could give Eli a safe place in which to relax and be himself, in which he could forget about his stressful day, then that was what he would do.

He rubbed Eli's back. "Everything okay?"

Eli nodded against Dorran's neck and stepped back. Dorran wanted to keep him there, but dinner was almost ready, and Eli needed to eat before he went to bed. He'd have to get up early tomorrow morning, just like he always did, so the sooner he went to bed, the better it would be for him. It wasn't the best thing, because they barely get the occasion to spend time together as a couple, but Dorran hoped they could be together during Eli's next off day. He had no way to know when that would happen, but it would eventually.

He kissed Eli's cheek and gestured toward the kitchen. "You're just in time for dinner."

Eli smiled. "I was hoping I would be."

Dorran rubbed the back of his neck. "It's not much."

"It doesn't matter. It's a home-cooked meal. That's more than good enough for me."

Dorran had prepared enough spaghetti for both of them. He always made sure Eli could have his share if he happened to come by. If he didn't, it would make leftovers for Dorran. He didn't have them often, though. Even when he was tired after a long day of work, Eli always tried to come by, even if it was only for dinner.

"My mother called," Eli said while they were eating.

Dorran froze for a second, then spun some spaghetti with his fork. "Yeah? What did she say?"

"She wanted to know about Sunday lunch."

Of course she did. Sunday lunch was important for Eli's

entire family. They tried to meet every week, although most of the time, at least one of them couldn't be there, usually Eli because of his job. That meant he and his family treasured the times he could go, although Dorran couldn't help but wonder if they still felt that way now that he usually accompanied Eli.

"She asked me if you're coming," Eli said. He was focused on his food, something for which Dorran was grateful.

He didn't want Eli to see his grimace. Hell, he didn't want to feel the way he did, but he couldn't change it.

He'd been angry when Eli's family, especially his mother, hadn't accepted him as Eli's boyfriend. He'd wanted them to, and he'd pushed for Eli to tell them they were a couple. Now Eli had, and things were changing, but Dorran couldn't help but feel unwelcome most of the time. It was mostly Eli's mother, and she was trying so hard. Dorran understood that, and he saw it. But he couldn't help how awkward things were when he went, and how uncomfortable she was. That meant he never wanted to go, even though he'd been the one pushing for it.

But things would never get better if Dorran didn't force himself to do this. He could stay home when Eli visited his family. Eli wouldn't push for him to go, and neither would Eli's family. But if Dorran wanted his relationship with Eli to last, it meant accepting that his family came with him and that Dorran had to deal with them. He hoped that in time, they'd be more comfortable around each other. He wanted to go back to the way things had been when he'd been a teenager and Eli's best friend. Of course, that had been before he and Eli had fallen in love—before they'd become a couple. Eli's parents hadn't known what kind of relationship Eli and Dorran were in then, but they did now.

Dorran cleared his throat. "Of course I'm coming. You don't even have to ask."

Eli arched a brow and put down his fork. He took Dorran's

hand and squeezed it. "I'll always ask. I know you don't feel great when we go, but—"

"That's not true," Dorran protested even though he knew it was a lie.

"Come on, Dorran. I know things are awkward. I'm there with you, remember? But I'm grateful for the fact that you're trying. I know my mother isn't making things easy for you, but that hasn't put you off yet, and I hope it won't. She's getting better, I promise."

Dorran leaned closer and kissed Eli. "I know. And I'll keep trying." Even though it wasn't easy. Even though Dorran felt like running away most of the time.

Besides, it wasn't that bad. Eli's father and his brothers treated Dorran the same way they had when Dorran had spent time with them all those years ago. Dorran didn't miss the way they sometimes hesitated when they'd talked about his and Eli's relationship, but it never lasted long. They were becoming Dorran's family just as much as his own siblings were, and that was good. Dorran could stand being awkward and uncomfortable for a while if it made Eli happy.

Still, he was grateful when Eli started talking about his cat and how she'd been misbehaving because he wasn't spending enough time with her. She was used to it, but Eli had always gone home at the end of the day before. Now, he wasn't, and Princess Butterfly wasn't happy.

After dinner, Dorran and Eli settled on the couch. They made out for a bit, but it didn't lead to anything more, and that was okay. They were past the first part of their relationship when they had to be in bed every second they spent together. They still had plenty of sex, but they were more relaxed, and they enjoyed spending time together like this, watching TV on the couch, making out and cuddling together. They weren't just boyfriends anymore. They weren't dating anymore, not only. They were settling in as a couple, in a routine, and it felt good.

Until Francis decided it would be a good idea to appear in the armchair.

Dorran tensed. He wasn't sure Eli could see Francis. He glared at Francis and looked up at Eli, trying to understand if he was aware of what was happening.

He was. His gaze flicked to the armchair, and he frowned. Dorran held his breath, expecting Eli to freak out. He would have before, but he didn't this time, and Dorran wasn't sure why. Instead of saying something, of telling Francis to get out, Eli turned his attention back to the TV. His arm around Dorran's shoulders tightened, but that was the only thing he did.

Maybe he was getting used to Francis' presence in their life. Maybe he was just too tired to say anything. Whatever the reason, Dorran hoped it meant Eli was finally coming to terms with Dorran's gifts and with Francis being a part of their life.

CHAPTER TWO

Dorran smiled when he felt the hand run up his side. He'd been surprised when Eli had told him he had today off last night over their spaghetti, but he was glad. He missed Eli, and Eli needed rest. He needed to be able to spend the day in bed, and Dorran was more than happy to put his work to the side. He could catch up over the weekend when Eli was working, although, of course, he'd have to make sure to keep most of Sunday free, since he and Eli were going to Sunday lunch.

Dorran snuggled his back against Eli's chest. Eli's hand moved to Dorran's stomach, his fingers tickling as he sought Dorran's cock.

He found it.

He wrapped his fingers around it, and Dorran groaned. He screwed his eyes shut, focusing on the feeling of Eli's hands on him and the pleasure he was so good at creating. He knew how to play Dorran's body. He always had, ever since those first fumbles under the sheets. But they weren't teenagers anymore, and Eli's hands were strong and sure as he touched Dorran.

Dorran pressed back against him, smiling when he felt Eli's hard cock pressed between his ass cheeks. Eli didn't push for more. Instead, he rubbed his cock against Dorran's body as he was jacking Dorran off. Dorran loved this kind of sleepy, warm sex. It was a great way to wake up, and he wanted that to happen every day for the rest of his life.

He groaned as he came, spilling over Eli's fist and the sheets. He'd have to change them, but then, he always did when Eli slept over. He'd had to buy two new sets of sheets because he was washing them so often.

Dorran slumped back against Eli, and Eli kissed the back of his neck. "Good morning," he rumbled.

Dorran smiled. "It certainly is. Are we spending the entire day in bed?"

"That sounds perfect. We might have to get up to eat something, though. Probably shower, too."

"I suppose we could." It wasn't like Dorran particularly liked being crusty anyway. It was a pity they couldn't share the shower, because it was so small, but Eli used the one in the guest room, and they finished at about the same time. They met in the living room for breakfast, and Dorran couldn't stop smiling. He hadn't expected a vacation day, but he'd make the most of it.

He was still thinking about what he and Eli could do with their day when someone knocked on the door. He and Eli looked at each other, and Eli arched a brow. "Were you expecting someone?"

"I wasn't. Maybe it's Emanuel." He and Dorran had become friends after Dorran had worked to prove he wasn't a killer. They usually spent at least an evening or two a week together, drinking beer and watching TV. Neither of them enjoyed sports, but it was fun to watch football and listen to Emanuel compare it to soccer.

Dorran abandoned his toast on his plate and went to the front door. He opened it and looked at the man standing on the other side. He didn't recognize him, even though he was vaguely familiar. "Yes?"

The man was staring at Dorran as if he'd seen a ghost, and it made Dorran uncomfortable. When he didn't answer, Dorran cleared his throat. "Can I help you?" he asked.

The man jerked. "Of course. I'm sorry. I was looking for Dorran Wells?"

"You found him." And he still hadn't told Dorran why he was there and why he was looking for him.

"Oh. Uh, my name is Angus Wells."

It took Dorran a moment to recognize the name. His father had died when he was three, and he barely remembered him. But his name had been Angus, and of course, they shared the same surname. "What a coincidence."

Wells shook his head. "It's not."

"Dorran?" Eli asked. "Is everything okay?"

Dorran was grateful when Eli came to stand behind him. He leaned against him, wondering why Wells made him feel unsettled. "I'm not sure."

Eli looked at Wells. "Did you need something?"

Dorran didn't miss the way Wells looked at Eli's arm around Dorran's waist. He was sure Eli had noticed it, too.

Wells shuffled. "I need to talk to Dorran alone," he said.

Dorran already knew that wasn't going to happen from the way Eli's arm tightened around him. "You can talk to both of us."

He'd step back if Dorran asked him to, but Dorran wasn't planning to. Whatever was happening, Dorran wasn't feeling good about it, and he doubted that was going to change.

Wells looked at Dorran. "Please?"

Dorran shook his head. "Eli is my boyfriend. You can speak in front of him. I'll tell him anything you're about to tell me anyway."

Dorran didn't know if Wells was homophobic, or just unused to seeing two men together, but he didn't like the flinch Wells gave when Dorran told him Eli was his boyfriend. He'd been unsettled before, but now he was getting angry, and he wanted this to be over — whatever *this* was.

"I see," Wells said. "All right. As I was telling you, the name isn't a coincidence. I *am* Angus Wells. And I'm your father."

Dorran snorted loudly. "That's not possible. My father died when I was three."

"I didn't. I didn't even know that was what your mother had told you."

Dorran didn't know how he felt. Right now, it was almost as if he wasn't in his body. Numb was probably the best way to describe it, but Dorran was also confused and getting angrier by the second. "Do you think you're funny? My father died when I was a kid."

Wells raised his hands. "I didn't. I'm right here, Dorran."

Dorran moved back, and to his relief, Eli stepped to the side so he could. Eli didn't leave, though. He stayed there, holding Dorran close as he glared at Wells. "Don't touch him," he snapped.

Wells looked annoyed. "This is why I want to talk to him alone. This is none of your business."

"It is when Dorran is my boyfriend. And don't you dare touch him without his consent, because I'll arrest your ass faster than you said *I'm your father*."

Wells took a step back. "I'm not here to hurt Dorran. I want to talk to him."

"I don't think he wants to talk to you."

Dorran hated the way they were talking about him as if he wasn't even there, but he couldn't seem to form one coherent thought, let alone say it out loud.

This man was familiar. Dorran couldn't deny that. It didn't mean he was his father, and Dorran didn't want to believe it. Why would his mother tell him his father had died when he hadn't? Why had she lied all these years? And why had his father left in the first place without letting Dorran and his siblings know he was alive? Dorran could understand why the man in front of him hadn't told him anything, since he'd only been three, but Bettany and Chris had been older. Hell, Chris had been seventeen, and he thought their father had died, too.

Wells looked a Dorran. "Please. I just want to explain what happened."

Dorran shook his head. He didn't know if he could believe this man, but he didn't want to. He wanted him to leave and never come back. "Leave me alone."

"Dorran, please."

But Dorran didn't want to listen to him. He moved away from the door, pulling Eli along, and as soon as he could, he slammed the door in Wells' face.

He couldn't breathe, or at least, that was what it felt like. He tried to suck in a breath, but his chest was tight.

Then strong arms wrapped around him, and Eli guided him toward the couch. "Sit down. Breathe, Dorran. Please."

Eli climbed onto the couch and slid behind Dorran's back. He pulled Dorran against him, holding him close, and Dorran forced himself to relax and to focus on the rhythm of Eli's breathing. He didn't know how long it took, but he finally managed to match it, and his lungs filled with air.

"What happened?" Francis asked.

Dorran didn't know how to answer. He wasn't sure he could.

"Dorran's father was at the door," Eli said.

Dorran would have probably startled if Eli had talked to Francis at any other time, but he couldn't feel anything right now.

"But his father is dead," Francis said.

"That's what he thought. That's what we both thought."

"You were wrong?"

"It looks like we might have been."

CHAPTER THREE

Dorran's thoughts were still jumbled. He'd been obsessively thinking about what had happened yesterday, and he couldn't seem to stop. The fact that Eli had found a note slipped under the door hadn't helped.

Dorran hadn't read it yet. He'd wanted to throw it away as soon as Eli found it, but Eli had suggested he not, and Dorran wasn't sure he would have been able to.

He wanted answers. He hadn't even known he was supposed to ask questions, and he hadn't — ever. It wasn't like his mother would have answered anyway. She told Dorran and his siblings that their father was dead for a reason, even though Dorran didn't know that reason. He could ask her, but even on their best days, it was hard for her to focus. The alcohol had ruined her, and most days, Dorran didn't want to see her. He forced himself to check in on her at least once a week and to go there once a month with Bettany to clean the apartment. Bettany still hoped their mom would get better.

Dorran didn't.

He knew their mother would never get better. She'd tried to stop drinking so many times without success that Dorran wouldn't allow himself to hope anymore. And now this.

What had happened? Why had his father left? And why had his mother told him his father was dead if he wasn't? Did she know he wasn't? Or had Angus disappeared without telling her anything?

Dorran didn't know what to think, but he was angry. That, he was sure of. He had no idea who he was angry with, though. Angus, for sure. With his mother, too. But what if she hadn't known? What if she'd started drinking because she thought the man she loved had died? That would explain why she'd never wanted to discuss him with Dorran.

God knew he'd asked. He'd grown up without a father. In the beginning, he hadn't cared. Then he'd realized that his school friends had both a mother and father, and he asked his mother why he didn't. Her answer had always been the same, and the only one she'd given him. His father had died when he was three.

That was it. She'd never told him what had happened. As far as he knew, she hadn't told Bettany and Chris either. Now the reason for so much secrecy made sense. Dorran had thought it was because his mother didn't want to think about it because it hurt too much. And maybe it did. Maybe that was why she'd started drinking. Dorran didn't know, because she'd never talked to him about it, and he doubted she had with Bettany or Chris.

He would ask them, though. He needed to. He had to tell them the man who said he was their father was there, that he wanted to talk to him, possibly to them, too. Dorran still had no idea if Angus Wells was his father or if he had a twisted sense of humor. He didn't know why the man had come. He didn't know if he wanted to talk to him.

He didn't know what to do.

Eli had left for work earlier that morning. Dorran had felt okay with him there, but now that he was alone in the apartment, he couldn't stop thinking about this. He hadn't even tried to work because he already knew he wouldn't be able to focus. His thoughts went around and around, always coming back to Angus Wells.

Was he really Dorran's father?

Dorran shook his head and pushed himself off the couch. He snagged his cell phone from the coffee table and quickly dialed Bettany's number before he could think better of it. He wasn't looking forward to having this conversation with her, but she deserved to know. They both deserved answers, and while Dorran didn't think she'd be able to give him those answers, talking to her was the first step.

He paused before hitting the green button. He needed to talk to Chris, too. The three of them needed to talk.

Instead of calling his sister, he went to the guest bedroom and turned his computer on. Then he organized a conference call so they could all three be there. He hoped they would answer, because he needed to talk to them.

He was lucky. They both did, although Chris was on his phone.

"Dorran? What's happening?" he asked.

Dorran couldn't help but smile. He and Chris had lost sight of each other for so long that Dorran hadn't thought they'd ever be able to get along again. But they had, even though it had taken Chris being accused of murdering his girlfriend for that to happen. Chris was still working through all of that, but he was better, and Dorran was glad he had his brother in his life again. "Nothing. Well, that's not exactly true, but I'm fine physically."

"You know that's not making us feel better, right?" Bettany asked.

Dorran didn't know how to tell them, so he decided to focus on his questions first. "I need to talk to the two of you about our father."

Chris blinked. "Our father?"

"Mom never told me what happened. I mean, I was only three at the time, and I don't remember him. I have no idea how he died. I asked her a few times, but she never answered."

Bettany frowned. "Why do you want to know?"

"Please?"

She bit her lower lip. "To be honest, I'm not sure, either. She spent a lot of time crying those days, and I was afraid of asking her what had happened. And after, well, you already know."

Dorran looked at Chris. "What about you? You were seventeen. That was old enough to understand." And to ask questions.

Chris grimaced. "She never told me. No matter how hard I tried to find out, I couldn't. I wish I had answers for you, but I don't."

"So how do either of you know he's dead?"

They were both shocked, but Bettany was the first one to recover. "Why are you asking that, Dorran? What happened?"

Dorran sighed and rubbed his forehead. He had to tell them. "A man came to my apartment yesterday. He said he was my father. *Our* father."

"But that's not possible. He's dead. He's been dead for twenty-five years."

Maybe Dorran should have read the note Angus had left. It might have given him answers he didn't have right now. He fingered it, but he still couldn't bring himself to open it. "That's what I thought, and to be honest, I don't know if this guy was serious. But I don't see any reason for him to lie. If only we knew more about what happened twenty-five years ago, maybe we could understand if this is the truth."

Chris grimaced. "I can't tell you how he died, but I'm pretty sure neither of you is aware of what happened back then, are you?"

Dorran almost yelled at his brother, but instead, he took a deep breath. "What do you mean? I don't know anything about that. I was only three."

"Okay. I came back one evening, the evening he died. Mom was at the kitchen table, and she was drinking."

Dorran sucked in a breath. He hadn't realized his mother had started drinking that early. It was a small miracle that she was still alive after twenty-five years of being an alcoholic.

"Dad wasn't there," Chris continued. "I asked her what happened, where he was, and she told me he was dead. I tried to push for answers, but she stopped and started yelling at me. I left her alone that night and stopped trying after a while, because it was obvious she wasn't going to tell me."

"There was no funeral," Bettany said slowly.

"You're right, there wasn't. I thought it was weird, but even though Dad never came back, I didn't think she'd lied. Why would she have?"

Dorran didn't know, but they had more questions than they'd had before.

"You should have told us," Bettany said. She sounded as angry as Dorran felt.

"I know. I'm sorry. But you know how things went."

"We should talk to Mom," Dorran said.

"She won't answer," Bettany said.

"Maybe not, but we need to try. She's the only one who can tell us." Except for Angus, but Dorran wasn't about to call him, not yet.

"I want to be there when you do," Chris said.

Dorran was grateful. He didn't think he could do this alone, and he couldn't ask Eli to be there. Eli had work, and he needed to focus on that. He would come if Dorran asked him to, but Dorran wouldn't, not yet. "We should meet tomorrow. We can talk, then go see her."

Bettany sighed heavily. "All right."

It was obvious neither of them wanted to do this, but they had to.

Dorran wished they didn't.

It was impossible. No matter how hard Dorran tried to

work, he couldn't focus on more than a few words at a time, which was a problem, since he was translating a medical text. He needed to be precise, and he couldn't right now.

He couldn't stop thinking about his father. He didn't even know if that man was who he'd said he was, but now Angus had put the thought in Dorran's mind, and Dorran couldn't focus on anything else.

His father was alive. Well, he probably was. Dorran couldn't think of a reason Angus would lie about that, so he was going with the assumption he wasn't. Which meant his father was alive, even though Dorran thought he died when he was three.

Dorran had no idea what to do with that. He had no idea how to *feel* about it.

He wanted to stop thinking about it. Focusing on his father and the situation wasn't helping, and it wouldn't. It wouldn't give Dorran more answers. For that, he had to visit his mother, which he was doing tomorrow with Bettany and Chris. He doubted they'd get answers, or at least, not the answers they wanted, but they had to try.

And Dorran had to try working right now.

He sighed and rubbed his forehead. He couldn't allow himself to mix up femur and tibia. Maybe he should take a break, even though he would feel guilty about it. He couldn't deny his situation was nothing he'd ever been in before. That wouldn't help him earning money, but he could afford to take a day or two off. Maybe it would be easier for him to focus once he knew what was going on. He didn't know what his mother would say, and knowing her, he doubted she'd be much help, but it would be something. It would be more than what he already had.

Dorran had never been so grateful when someone knocked on the door. He stumbled on his way out of his office and ignored Francis' chuckle. He swung the door open, blinking at

Carole. "Did we have an appointment I forgot about?"

She chuckled. "We did."

Dorran wasn't surprised he'd forgotten about it, considering everything that was going on.

He stepped aside to let Carole in, glaring at the ghost following her. "What is she doing here?" he asked.

Carole shrugged. "I thought you might want to take care of her yourself. You know, to practice."

Dorran wouldn't be against kicking Carole's aunt's ass out of his apartment, since she was a transphobic bitch, but he really could have done without having to listen to her berate Carole and using the wrong pronouns to talk about her. She always did, and Dorran hated it.

But since he had to do it, he might as well do it now so she wouldn't disturb the rest of the training session.

Dorran couldn't believe how easy it was to do this now. It hadn't been a few months ago, and he hadn't been sure he could do this. But he could, and he didn't even have to close his eyes to push Carole's aunt away. He looked her straight in the eyes as he did so. She opened her mouth, no doubt to scold him, but she was gone the next second, and nothing came out.

"Thank you for that. It's become easier, hasn't it?" Carole asked.

Dorran flopped onto the couch. "It has. I guess I'm ready for the next level? What else do you have to teach me?"

Carole hesitated. She sat in the armchair Dorran was starting to think of as hers and leaned her fingers together on her knee. Dorran wasn't sure why she was behaving this way, but he could tell it was important to her, so he stayed quiet.

She cleared her throat. "Honestly, I don't have anything else to teach you, not if you want to stick to being able to ignore ghosts and push them away."

That wasn't what Dorran had expected to hear. "Really?"

It was true it was easy for him now to push Carol's aunt away and to communicate with Francis, but he'd expected to have so much more to learn.

"When it comes to this, yes. But you can learn more."

Dorran nodded slowly. "What do you mean?"

She tapped her fingers on her thigh. "I know we never really talked about this, but you know I have a shop, right?"

"I do." From the little she'd told him it was a small place. She mostly worked with families who wanted to communicate with their dead, which Dorran admired.

"I've been getting a lot of business lately. The shop is doing well."

"And instead of working there, you're here helping me. I get it. I understand why you think this needs to stop. It's okay."

Carole shook her head. "That's not what I was trying to say. What I mean is that I could use help at the shop."

It took Dorran a moment to understand. "You want me to work with you?"

"I would love you to. You have a gift, and it's strong. I understand you haven't had a lot of time to deal with this or to think about it, but you would make good money if you worked for me. Hell, if things work out, I'm even ready to make you partner in the shop. I like you, Dorran. I trust you, and I want to work with you. I think we could do great things."

Dorran shook his head. He understood what Carole was saying, but he couldn't think about this now. He loved his job. He loved taking words in a language and making it so that people who didn't speak that language could understand them. He loved thinking about ways to make those words fit what they initially said. He also loved being able to work from home and set his own timetable. He doubted Carole would expect him to sit at the shop from nine to four, but still. It wouldn't be the same."

"You don't have to give me an answer right now, of course," Carole said. "I know this is a surprise for you, and that you have a job and a boyfriend to think of."

If only she knew what Dorran was dealing with. He could tell her, and she would understand, but he didn't want to. He had no idea how he felt about Angus being back in his life and his mother lying to him for more than twenty-five years. He didn't want to dump that kind of problem on Carole. They were friends, but not close enough for him to feel comfortable with this.

And he wasn't sure he'd be comfortable with working with her.

It had nothing to do with her and everything to do with him. He'd never known he had this power, this gift. He hadn't suspected it until he'd first seen Francis. He wasn't sure he wanted it. It was fun to be able to talk to Francis, and he knew Francis was relieved someone could see him, but Dorran could do without everything else. He didn't want to have to listen to Carol's aunt ranting at her. He didn't want to see his brother's dead girlfriend. He wanted to focus on his books and his relationship with Eli.

Eli. God, he wouldn't be happy about this. It wasn't that he didn't like Carole, although Dorran knew they hadn't spent a lot of time together. But he *definitely* didn't like Dorran's gift, and if Dorran started working with Carole, he wouldn't be happy. Of course, that was without considering the fact that what Dorran did would be reflected on Eli at his job. His colleagues would find it hilarious that Eli's boyfriend worked as a psychic. Most of them didn't know about ghosts being real. Dorran was sure of that. *He* hadn't known until recently.

But he did know now. He knew, but he wasn't sure what to do about it. He realized he could help people find peace. He just wasn't sure he wanted to do that. His job was to translate, not to talk to ghosts. The only spirit he wanted to talk to was Francis. He wasn't interested in any other, except for the possibility to push them away and make sure they didn't invade his life.

"Dorran?" Carole sounded hesitant in a way she hadn't since they'd first met. Dorran didn't like it. He'd thought they were friends, and they were, but she didn't sound like it right now.

He smiled at her. "I'll think about it, okay?"

She smiled. "Of course. I told you, I never expected you to give me an answer right away. I know you already have a job and that Eli isn't happy about all this. So think about it and let me know." She scrunched her nose. "And I know there's something else. I can tell, even though you won't explain, and again, that's okay. I just want you to know I'm here if you need to talk."

"Of course." But Dorran suspected he would turn her down, and he couldn't help but feel guilty about that and that she was trying to be his friend while he would turn her offer down.

CHAPTER FOUR

Dorran saw Chris before Chris saw him. He slowed down, wanting to look at his brother. They hadn't seen each other in a while, but Chris looked happy. Dorran knew how hard things had been for him when his girlfriend had been killed, and he was glad Chris seemed to be recovering from that and from being arrested for her murder. He hadn't done anything, and he'd lost so much because of one man's hate and mistakes and lies. He didn't deserve this. He didn't deserve to be pulled into this family drama, but here he was, and Dorran knew they'd support each other. He and Chris hadn't been in contact for years, but now they were, and Dorran wouldn't change that for anything.

Chris looked up and noticed Dorran. He smiled at him, and Dorran smiled back. They were family, and they would face this as one.

Chris shuffled when Dorran got to him. "Hey. I haven't seen Bettany yet."

Dorran chuckled. "She's usually late. Having two kids will do that to you." Dorran realized what he'd said too late. He grimaced, but Chris shook his head.

"It's okay. You can talk about Bettany's children," Chris said.

Dorran thought it would be better if he didn't. Chris hadn't merely lost his girlfriend. He'd lost the baby she'd been expecting, and he was still working through this loss. "You look good," he said instead.

Chris grinned and shrugged. "I had been doing okay. I

could have done without this drama, but it is what it is."

"Trust me. I could have done without it, too."

"It must have been a shock when he told you. He was at your apartment, right?"

"He was. I didn't recognize him."

Chris snorted. "Of course you didn't. You were three when he left. You couldn't have remembered him. I'm surprised he decided to go to you rather than me or Bettany."

"I'm not. I mean, think about it. I was in shock, but he knows I was too young to remember him. That means I wouldn't be angry at him, not as much as you and Bettany might have been. He probably thought I was his best chance to explain what had happened."

"But he didn't tell you, right?"

"That's probably because I slammed the door in his face."

Chris laughed and gave Dorran a sideways hug.

It startled Dorran, because their family had never been touchy-feely, but it felt good.

"I want in on that hug, too," Bettany said, appearing and throwing herself at Dorran and Chris. They wrapped her in their arms, and Dorran took a moment to savor this.

Whatever happened, whatever their mother told them and whatever had happened with their father, they would always have this. They were a family, even without their parents. That wouldn't change.

Still, Dorran wasn't looking forward to this, and he knew neither were Chris and Bettany. They went straight to their mother's apartment, and Dorran hoped Chris was steeling himself. He hadn't been back in years, while Dorran and Bettany had been taking care of her. Dorran didn't hold that against Chris, especially not after everything that had happened. God knew he'd get out of this if he could.

But he couldn't. Not taking care of his mother anymore would leave everything to Bettany, and there was no way she was stepping out of that. No matter what their mother said or did to her, she thought it was her duty to take care of her, and nothing would stop her. That meant Dorran had to support her, and hopefully Chris, too, now that he was in the picture again.

But they could do this without him. They had for years, and that wouldn't change.

Chris rubbed the back of his neck as they walked out of the elevator. "I can't say I'm eager to do this," he confessed.

"None of us are. But it needs to be done," Dorran told him.

"I know it does. I want answers from both of them. But Bettany has been telling me about Mom and what's going on with her, and I don't want to see her that way. Not that I'm surprised this is how things ended, not after the way she reacted when Dad died." He paused. "Or left. Whatever."

"I suppose we're about to find out," Dorran said.

The three of them stopped in front of the front door and looked at each other. Dorran didn't knock. He never did, and neither did Bettany. Instead, he unlocked the door, opened it, and called out, "Mom?"

She never answered, but at least this way, she knew someone was in the apartment with her. She probably wouldn't have heard the knock, but she did hear Dorran. Dorran knew where he'd find her, even this early in the morning. He went straight to the living room, and sure enough, she was there, in her favorite armchair. There was a half-empty bottle of whiskey on the table next to her. It was open, and Dorran briefly closed his eyes and breathed in and out before reaching for it and closing it.

That got his mom's attention. She rolled her head and glared at him, but he ignored her. Instead, he handed the bottle to Bettany, who took it away. He didn't know where she'd hide it, and it didn't matter because their mother would find it anyway, but for now, they could have a conversation that didn't include their mom sipping on whiskey.

Dorran crouched in front of her armchair. "Mom? Chris is here." She hadn't seen him in a very long time, but she didn't seem to care.

She looked at Chris, but she didn't say anything. Chris, on the other hand, stepped closer. Dorran could read his expression well. He had never been in his brother's place. He'd been there as his mother declined and started drinking more and more, so he didn't have anything to compare her right now to how she'd been years ago. But he knew how different she was. Alcohol had taken its toll, and it would continue to. It was a small miracle that she was decently healthy and still alive.

"Hey, Mom," Chris said.

"What you want?" she asked. Her words were barely slurred, but it didn't mean she wasn't drunk. She probably hadn't downed a lot of whiskey that morning, but Dorran wouldn't be surprised if the bottle had been full last night.

Chris looked taken aback, and Dorran decided to take the lead. "I got a visit the other day. A man came to talk to me. He told me he was my father, Angus Wells."

"You told us he was dead," Chris said.

She narrowed her eyes. "Yes."

"That's not true," Dorran said. He couldn't be a hundred percent sure Angus was his father, but his mother would continue denying it unless he showed her that he didn't believe her.

She groaned and tried to get up, but she couldn't, and she flopped back into the armchair. "He should have."

There it was. "You think our father should have died?"

"He ruined my life."

So Angus probably was Dorran, Chris, and Bettany's father. Dorran had already suspected that, but hearing it from his mother wasn't easy. "How?" How could he have ruined her life so much that she told his children he was dead?

"He wanted to leave," she snapped.

Dorran blinked and looked at Chris, who shrugged. He didn't seem to know any more than Dorran did, even though he'd been seventeen at the time. "Leave?" Dorran asked.

"Divorce. He wanted a divorce."

"And what did you do?" How had they gone from wanting a divorce to him being fake-dead?

"I kicked him out, of course."

"And you told us he was dead," Chris finished.

Dorran didn't want to know why she'd done it. He thought it was obvious, and the last thing he wanted right now was to have to deal with her tears.

His father had wanted a divorce. Whatever the reason behind that, it didn't matter. What did matter was the way his mother had reacted. Instead of accepting it, or even trying to fight it, she'd kicked him out and had told his children he was dead.

Dorran had no idea why Angus hadn't tried contacting him and his siblings, or why he hadn't fought for them. But he had his answers.

The three of them did.

"I don't know what to think about this," Bettany said as they left the apartment.

Their mother was safe, still sitting in her armchair, watching TV. She'd probably get up any second to try to find her bottle of whiskey, but Dorran didn't care. He was past that. He'd worried and hoped for too long to still care.

"Why didn't he ever contact us?" he asked. He didn't expect an answer, and he knew his brother and sister weren't the ones who could answer his question.

"We won't know until we talk to him."

But Dorran still wasn't sure he wanted to. He had no idea

why Angus had reached out to him instead of Bettany or Chris, because they would remember him. Maybe he was right, and Angus had been afraid they'd be too angry to talk to him. He'd misjudged it, though, because Dorran was just as angry. But Bettany was willing to give Angus a chance, and Dorran didn't know if he could do that.

He didn't know what life with a father was like. He'd never had that. He didn't know what he'd lost, and he wasn't sure he wanted to find out. What kind of relationship could he and Angus have? He'd abandoned Dorran, Chris, and Bettany. Dorran had never known him, and he didn't have a reason to want to now. Chris and Bettany might want to see if they could patch things up, but Dorran had nothing to patch up.

"Why don't we get that coffee we were supposed to drink before doing this?" Chris asked.

Dorran was grateful for the distraction.

None of them talked until they were sitting at a table in the coffee shop. The silence between them was heavy with questions and hesitation, and Dorran wasn't sure how to break it. He didn't know what else there was to say.

"You have his phone number?" Bettany asked.

Dorran didn't have to ask to know who she was talking about. "I do." He'd finally opened the note Angus had left under his door. There hadn't been much to it, just Angus' full name and his phone number, and an apology. Dorran wanted a lot more, but he knew he wouldn't get it until he talked to Angus, and he wasn't ready for that.

But Bettany might be.

"Can you give it to me?" she asked.

"Of course. What are you going to do? Will you talk to him? Will you ask him what really happened?"

She rotated her coffee cup with both hands, looking down at it. "I don't know. I want his number so I can call him if I feel like it, but I don't know if that will ever happen. But I want answers. I think the three of us deserve them."

"I don't want anything from him," Chris snapped.

His reaction took Dorran aback. "Not even to talk to him?" Dorran understood his own reasons behind not wanting to do it, but Chris had been seventeen when their father had left. He'd had a relationship with him. Didn't he want that to happen again? Didn't he want to fix things?

"No."

"Not even to get answers?" Bettany asked softly.

"I don't want answers. I don't care why he left or why he wanted to divorce Mom. The only thing I care about is that he abandoned us. He left us behind without worrying about what happened to us. I mean, he wanted a divorce for a reason, right?"

"Had she already started drinking before that?" Dorran asked. Even though he didn't want to see Angus, it didn't mean he didn't want to know what had happened.

Chris sighed heavily and slumped back in his chair. "Yeah. She was drinking, and she wasn't always pleasant to be around. That's why I spent as much time as I could out of the house. But I was a kid. He wasn't, and he should have thought about us before going. He should have fought for us."

"But he didn't." That was what Dorran had a problem with.

He might be able to understand why Angus had left. There were some problems that couldn't be solved and for which divorce was the best option. He didn't blame Angus for wanting that. But he did blame him for not looking back—for not caring enough about his kids to make sure they were okay. He'd left them with their mother even though he knew she was a drunk. Dorran wasn't sure he would ever be able to forgive that. Chris certainly didn't look like he could.

Bettany huffed. "Well, you don't have to talk to him if you don't want to. But I do. I want to ask him why he wanted to divorce mom in the first place. I want to know why he didn't try to help us, and why he didn't try to contact us over the years. I want to know why he decided to do that now."

She wasn't wrong. Dorran was curious about that, too.

Why was Angus here now? He knew where Dorran lived. Besides, even if he hadn't, it wouldn't have been hard to find. Dorran's mother still lived in the apartment she and Angus had shared. It was too big for her, but it was hers. Angus could have found her easily, and from there, he would have found Dorran, Bettany, and Chris.

So why had he waited? Why was he here now?

Dorran wanted to know, too, but he didn't think he was up to talking to Angus, not yet. He wanted some time to think about what he'd found out, wrap his mind around it. Maybe Bettany was ready for more, but Dorran wasn't.

"Will you tell us if you get answers from him?" he asked. Because while he didn't want to talk to Angus, he did want to know what had happened.

Bettany smiled softly. She looked sad, while Chris was pissed. "Of course I will. I understand why you don't want to talk to him, you know? I'm not looking forward to it, either. Whatever happened between him and Mom, he still abandoned us. But I want to find out if there was a reason for that. You know Mom. You know how awful she can be. I'm not surprised he wanted a divorce."

"Even so, he shouldn't have left us behind," Chris said.

"You're right, he shouldn't have, and I'm planning on asking him why he did. I'm not saying I want a relationship with him. I don't know if I do. But I do want to know what happened. I want him to look me in the eyes and tell me why he abandoned us." Bettany sounded convinced, and Dorran was impressed.

He was also worried. He didn't want his sister to get hurt, and he was afraid that was what would happen. But she wanted to give Angus a chance to at least explain. Dorran couldn't say no to that. Bettany was an adult. She was older than Dorran. She had her own life, her own thoughts, and she knew what she could stand and what she could deal with.

If she thought this was the best way for her to come to terms with what was happening, Dorran had no say in it. But he'd be there for her if she needed him.

He had to start thinking about what he wanted, though. Angus wasn't leaving, not yet, maybe not ever. Dorran knew nothing about why he was here and for how long, but there was a reason, and he doubted Angus would leave until he got what he wanted.

Whatever that was.

CHAPTER FIVE

"Pass the salad?" Eli asked.

Dorran smiled at him. "You must like it if you're taking a second serving."

Eli shrugged, but Dorran didn't miss the smile on his face. "So what if I like it?"

"Nothing. I'm just not used to seeing you eat green stuff."

"I eat vegetables," Eli muttered.

Dorran looked down at his plate. He enjoyed teasing Eli, and he liked it even more when Eli played with him, too. "Well, I can't deny salad is a vegetable, but you should probably try to branch out. How about I cook some broccoli for tomorrow's dinner?"

Eli grimaced. "I hate broccoli. It smells like feet."

Dorran laughed. "I can't deny its smelly, but that doesn't mean it's not tasty. Trust me? I promise I won't force you to eat it if you don't want to, but I'd like you to try."

Eli glared, but he nodded, and Dorran knew he'd won. It was satisfying. Eli trusted Dorran enough to eat broccoli. Wasn't that the pinnacle of love?

"I meant to ask about your father," Eli said.

Dorran's happiness took a dive. "Why?" He was tempted to stonewall Eli and ignore his questions about Angus, but he wouldn't do that. He expected Eli to be okay with him worrying over him, and the same went the other way. Eli was worried about him, which was the only reason he was asking that. He wasn't on Angus' side. He was on Dorran's, and that meant a lot.

"I just want to know you're okay." Eli reached out and took Dorran's hand, squeezing. "You haven't talked about it a lot, even though I know you've met with Bettany and Chris and that you've talked to your mother. I didn't want to push, and I still don't. But you know I'm here if you need to talk. I'll listen to you and try to work things out with you if that's what you need. I just don't think you should keep everything inside. Bottling things up isn't good."

Dorran sighed and put his fork down. "You're right, it's not. I don't have a lot to tell you. It's true that Bettany, Chris, and I talked to our mother, but she didn't have a lot to say."

"She still insists he's dead?"

"She admitted she kicked him out because he wanted a divorce. That's all we got from her, though. Bettany asked for Angus' phone number to talk to him, but she hasn't called me yet. I don't know if she's talked to him." He didn't know anything more.

"What do you want?"

Dorran had had time to think about that. It had been a few days since he and his sibs had visited their mother. They hadn't talked yet, but Dorran had come to a conclusion. "I want to know what happened. I mean, I believe my mother when she says my father wanted a divorce and that she kicked him out. It sounds exactly like something she would do in that situation. I also wouldn't be surprised to find out that Angus wanted to divorce her because she was drinking. But that doesn't tell me why he left me, Bettany, and Chris behind. He was our father, and it feels like he didn't even fight for us. Instead, he left us with our mother even though he knew she drank."

"But you don't know that."

Dorran frowned. "I don't know what?"

"You don't know that he left you behind, or that he didn't fight for you. I mean, he and your mother divorced. Do you know how that went? Why he didn't have at least the weekends with you? Or why he didn't try contacting you once you were adults? I understand you're angry and feel abandoned, but you don't have all the information."

Dorran wanted to snap, but Eli was right. Dorran didn't know anything about the divorce, and he wouldn't be surprised if his mother had found a way to keep him and his siblings away from their father to spite him and to get revenge.

She was angry at him still. It had been almost thirty years, but she still hated him and blamed him for the way her life had gone. She would never admit her own choices had made her what she was now, even though that was the truth.

But Dorran understood. He understood why his father had wanted a divorce. *He* wanted to run away from his mother most days, but especially so when he had to spend any length of time with her. It still hurt because it felt like he'd been abandoned, and he was still angry at being lied to for years.

This last thing had nothing to do with his father, though.

Angus had left, but he wasn't responsible for what Dorran's mother had done. He wasn't responsible for the lies. He wasn't responsible for them thinking he was dead.

Dorran wasn't sure he would ever be able to get over everything else, but that was one thing he couldn't put at his father's feet.

"Why don't we go to bed?" Eli asked as he rose from his chair. "I can give you a massage so you'll relax. I know a good night's sleep won't solve all your problems, but you'll feel better."

Dorran wasn't sure anything could make him feel better right now, but he wanted to spend time with Eli. He wanted to forget about his mother and his father for a while. He needed to forget—not to think about them and obsess over the reasons behind what they'd done and said.

He and Eli cleaned up the kitchen together, mostly silent.

Dorran couldn't help but smile at the way Eli kept brushing against him, though. It wasn't sexual, even though he wouldn't have protested that. But Eli was showing him he was there, that he would come for him and be there for him if he needed him.

And Dorran did. He had his brother and his sister, and they were the most involved in this situation, but it helped to have someone who didn't have a stake in this. Eli didn't care whether Dorran chose to talk to his father or not. He didn't care if Dorran decided never to go to see his mother again. He only wanted Dorran to be happy, and that was what Dorran needed. Eli didn't have hidden motives about the situation, or motives at all. He was the perfect sounding board, and Dorran would use him that way, but not now.

Now, he wanted his massage.

He stripped down to his underwear when he and Eli got to the bedroom. Eli guided him toward the bed, and Dorran settled on his stomach and closed his eyes. He listened to Eli move around the bedroom, opening and closing a drawer. Then Eli climbed onto the bed and settled on Dorran's ass.

He was still wearing his underwear, too, but Dorran could feel the hair on Eli's legs prickle against his skin. He'd ditched the jeans, and probably his t-shirt, too. That way, he wouldn't get oil on them.

It wasn't the first time this happened, although usually, their roles were reversed. Eli was the one who needed to be relaxed more than Dorran in their everyday life. Dorran loved giving him that, helping him.

And now Eli was helping him.

Dorran groaned when Eli started digging his thumbs into the muscles in his back. He hadn't realized how tense he was until now, and he hated that this was a result of the situation with his parents. He wanted all of that to stop, but since that wasn't possible, he could push it away at least for an evening.

Eli kissed the back of Dorran's neck. "Just like this. Stop thinking about that. That situation isn't going anywhere. It will be there tomorrow when you have to think about it again, but for now, push it out."

Someone chuckled. "Maybe you should push *in*."

Dorran groaned, but it wasn't in pleasure this time. "Francis. You need to leave."

"And here I thought I was about to get a show."

Eli grunted and rolled off Dorran. For one second, Dorran thought he was going to dress and leave, but instead, he maneuvered both of them until they were under the blankets. They were still oily, and Dorran would have to change his sheets tomorrow, but that was okay because he was with Eli, cuddled against his chest. Instead of going away at this sign of Dorran's gift and the fact that ghosts existed, Eli was staying.

"You're not going to sleep, are you?" Francis asked.

"Shut it and go to the living room," Eli told him, stunning Dorran, and probably Francis, too.

"Well, I can't say I expected this. Good for you, though. I'm glad to see your family is finally accepting me."

Eli grumbled something against the skin of Dorran's neck, but Dorran didn't understand what, and he didn't ask. It was enough for him that Eli seemed to be accepting this.

For now.

CHAPTER SIX

"You should call him," Eli said as he knotted his tie.

Dorran buried his face into his pillow. He knew who Eli was talking about, of course, and he was thinking about it. But his first instinct was to say no and to push Angus away as far as he could. He didn't want to talk to either of his parents right now.

But he did want to know what had happened.

He sighed. "I don't want to."

Eli smoothed his tie down and turned to look at Dorran. "You do. You just don't want to admit it."

Dorran glared. "How do you know me so well?"

Eli chuckled and sat on the mattress next to Dorran's hip. He rubbed Dorran's back, and Dorran closed his eyes, enjoying the contact. He wanted more. He wanted Eli to stay home with him, but that wasn't possible. They were both adults, and they needed to go to work. Well, Eli did. Dorran would certainly try, but he still wasn't sure he could focus long enough to get even a few chapters translated.

"I know you so well because we met when we were kids," Eli said.

"But we were separated for years."

"You're right, but that doesn't mean you've changed so much that I don't know you anymore. I do. I know that your first instinct is to say no and stand your ground. You don't want to give either of your parents more room to hurt you, and I get it. I can't even imagine what you're going through right now. My family might not be the easiest to get along

40

with, but we love each other. I've always known that."

Dorran grabbed Eli's pillow and hugged it. "I don't understand why he's here," he murmured.

"And you won't understand it until you ask him. You don't have to make any promises. Call him, ask him why he came back now, what he wants, and make your decision once you have all the information you need. No one expects you to welcome him with open arms. I don't think he expects that, either. He knows why you're being reluctant, and hopefully, he won't push too hard. But if he does, call me."

Dorran couldn't help but smile. "And what are you going to do? Threaten to arrest him?"

"If that's what it takes, sure."

Dorran felt better. He knew no one would push him to contact Angus if he didn't want to. No one would be surprised if he didn't. He could get all the information he wanted through Bettany, and that would be okay.

"Just think about it," Eli said. He rubbed Dorran's back one last time and got up. "I know this might not be what you want to hear, but this is your chance to have a relationship with your father. It can be whatever kind of relationship you want to have with him, but to make a decision, you need to know what's going on."

"I need all the information. I know. You already said that." That was the detective in Eli. He always wanted to know everything.

"You do. And once you have it, you can choose. You can tell him to fuck off and never come back. You can tell him you will call him every so often. You can see him once a week if that's what you want. I just hope you'll think about this. Don't throw a possible relationship with him away just because you're stubborn and you know you're in the right. You are. No one is denying that. But I'm sure your father has a reason to be here right now."

"You just want to know why he's here," Dorran teased.

The slight blush on Eli's cheeks told Dorran he was right. "I want you to be happy, whatever that entails."

Dorran knew that. Eli wasn't afraid anymore. He wanted Dorran to be happy, and he wanted Dorran to be happy with *him*. If that meant he had to spend the weekends with Dorran's father, he would.

Eli kissed the top of Dorran's head. "Call me if anything happens."

"You know I will. You already know what time you'll be home tonight?"

"No idea. I have to go to my apartment to feed the cat, and I'll have to see what my workload is. I'll let you know."

"And I'll text you after I call Angus. I'll let you know what happened."

It still took Dorran a good fifteen minutes to drag himself out of bed. He was usually an easy riser, and he knew the reason he'd lingered in bed this morning was that he was trying to waste time. He might want to know why Angus hadn't tried to reach out to him and his siblings earlier, but that didn't mean he was looking forward to having that conversation with him.

Seeing his father hurt. There was no way around that. It reminded Dorran of his childhood, of the life he'd had with his mother. It reminded him of how his mother had lied to him for most of his life. It wasn't the first time she disappointed him, but this might be the worst thing she'd ever done. Of course, Dorran wouldn't know until he talked to Angus, so he forced himself to grab his cell phone after breakfast and dialed the number that was still on the note Angus had left under the door.

"Angus Wells," he answered after a few rings.

Dorran took a deep breath. "It's Dorran."

Angus' tone softened. "I wasn't sure I'd hear from you."

"I'll be honest. It was a close thing. I'm still not sure I'm doing what's best for me, but I want answers."

"And I'll give you all the answers you need. I promise. I'm done holding back."

Dorran wanted to ask why he was holding back, but he didn't. "Good."

"I could come to your apartment."

Dorran might want to hear what Angus had to say, but he didn't want him in his home, not yet, maybe not ever. He didn't trust Angus, and he didn't know what would happen or if Angus would be part of his life after today. "How about we meet at a coffee shop? We can have a drink and take our time."

There was a hint of disappointment when Angus answered, but Dorran didn't care. "Of course. Just tell me when and where, and I'll be there."

"I'll text you the address."

Dorran was wary of having Angus anywhere near the apartment, even though Angus already knew where it was. He had conflicting feelings about this meeting. He was eager to end this and get answers to his questions, but he wasn't looking forward to getting hurt. Because that was what would happen. He already knew that.

Even if Dorran decided to welcome Angus into his life, even if Angus hadn't left because he wanted to, it would hurt. Dorran didn't have a great relationship with his mother. He never had. But she was still his mother, and he'd been taking care of her ever since he was a teenager and Bettany had left home. He had no clue whether the reason was that his mother would be alone, or that Bettany would carry the burden by herself—he just knew he wouldn't stop. All of which meant that whatever Angus told him, Dorran would have to accept it and put it aside when it came to his mother.

He wasn't sure he could do that.

But as Eli had said, this was his occasion to have a relationship with his father. He'd never thought he'd have one. He'd thought his father was dead for his entire life, and now he'd found out Angus wasn't.

Dorran didn't know what to do with a father. He didn't know if things would work. He didn't even know if he wanted a father. He was thirty. He had his own apartment, a job he loved, and a boyfriend. There might not be a place in his life for Angus.

Or maybe there was. Dorran wouldn't know until he talked to Angus, so after hanging up with him and texting him the address to one of his favorite coffee shops, he started getting ready. He could feel Francis watching him, even though the ghost was invisible right now. Francis was no doubt worried, but he didn't try to stop Dorran.

Dorran was grateful. He felt like anything—even a word—might make him decide to stay home. He didn't want to be a coward. He needed to face this, and he needed to face it now.

Dorran bounced his knee. He couldn't look away from the coffee shop door, and he doubted he would until Angus arrived. He shouldn't have come early, but he hadn't wanted to stay home. The last thing he needed was more time to obsess over what was happening. Except that here he was, obsessing over it even though he wasn't home. He couldn't win.

Maybe he should leave. Maybe wanting answers wasn't worth feeling as bad as he did right now. What would knowing what had happened change anyway?

Dorran sighed. It would change everything. He realized Angus had at least some fault in this situation. Even if he hadn't been able to take Dorran and his siblings with him when he'd left or to reach out to them later, he could have waited until they were adults. Yet Chris was forty-five, and he hadn't heard from Angus ever since he was seventeen.

Angus had had all the time he needed to contact Chris, yet he hadn't. Instead, he'd found Dorran.

Dorran hoped this wouldn't put a wedge between him and his brother. If he had to choose, he'd choose Chris.

But he didn't want to choose. He still wasn't sure what would happen with his father, but Eli was right. This was a chance to have a relationship with him and to find out what had happened, and Dorran didn't want to waste it. He also didn't want to lose his brother to it, though.

The coffee shop door opened, and Dorran jerked when he saw Angus walk in. He knew his father was in his late sixties, but he looked younger. There was a spring in his step and the smile that spread over his face when he saw Dorran helped, too.

Dorran raised a hand and gave a little wave. Angus gestured at the counter, and Dorran nodded. He'd already grabbed a coffee because he didn't think he could do this without something to hold onto. He probably should have skipped the caffeine, but it was too late for that now.

He wrapped both hands around his coffee cup and waited for Angus. He watched as his father settled in the chair across from him—then they stared at each other for a moment.

It was awkward. It was horrible. Dorran didn't know how to feel about it.

He sighed. "Well? Here I am, and I'm ready to listen."

Angus nodded. "I wasn't sure you would. I have to admit I'm nervous."

Dorran snorted. "Trust me. It's nothing next to how I feel."

Angus grimaced. "I can't believe Regina told you I was dead."

"But she did. She made me and my siblings believe you were dead for close to thirty years. You can understand how uncomfortable the three of us feel."

"I do. Bettany called me. Thanks for giving her my

number."

Dorran shrugged. "She asked for it. I might not be sure what I want to happen between you and me, but I wouldn't deny her. She wants to get to know you. I don't know if I share her belief that you had a good reason to abandon us, but I'm willing to listen."

Angus nodded. "That's all I'm asking for. I realize how hard this has to be for you and how confusing. I don't expect anything from you."

"You wouldn't be here if you didn't expect anything from me."

"I won't deny I hope you'll listen to me and that we eventually have a good relationship. But I know you won't forgive me easily, and honestly, I wouldn't either if I were in your shoes. I just—please just listen, okay? You can leave after I'm done if that's what you want, and I won't try to stop you."

Dorran was grateful he'd thought about doing this in a public place. He didn't think Angus would hurt him, but it was nice to have the buffer of people talking around them.

He nodded at Angus and waited for his father to explain.

Angus took a sip of his coffee and looked away from Dorran. "I'm aware you've talked to your mother, so you already know part of what happened."

"She only said that you wanted a divorce and that you left her."

"I did. We were young when we met in high school. We weren't high school sweethearts, but we might as well have been. We'd known each other for several years when things started changing between us and we got together."

"You had Chris when Mom was twenty-three. That's not young."

"You're right. It's not. I don't know if she ever told you that she got pregnant before Chris, though. That's one of the reasons we got married. She lost the baby when she was five months along."

Dorran hadn't known that. He felt like he didn't know either of his parents, and he hated it. No matter how hard life was with his mother, it was familiar, and in a way, reassuring. Or at least it had been until Angus had made him realize how much his mother had lied to him.

"We loved each other back then. I was happy when she got pregnant with Chris, then Bethany."

"But not when she did with me?"

Angus rubbed his face with his hand. "I'm sure you already know you were an unexpected baby. Your mother was almost forty when she got pregnant with you, and we thought we were done with babies. We'd already started drifting apart by then. Our love had changed, as it was bound to do. I mean, you've been in relationships. You know that the honeymoon phase doesn't last forever. You settle into a different kind of love, one that's closer to friendship. The problem with your mother was that in the end, it was all I felt for her. Friendship. I took my time thinking things over and making a decision because I didn't want to hurt her, and I didn't want to hurt you and your siblings. I thought I was doing the right thing when I told her I wanted a divorce, and I still do."

"What went wrong?" Dorran croaked.

"I didn't realize how she would react. I expected anger and sadness, of course. I'm sure I wasn't the only one who realized our relationship was changing and that it would be better for everyone to separate. That didn't mean I wouldn't be in your life, or at least, it shouldn't have meant that. But Regina got so angry when I told her. She kicked me out." Angus sucked in a breath. "Then, when we got in front of the judge and I thought I was going to see you and your siblings at least over the weekends, Regina told him that I was cheating on her and that she was afraid for her safety and yours. She didn't outright tell him I was abusive, but she made it sound like it, and no matter how much I protested, the judge agreed with her."

Dorran leaned back in his chair. He felt like he'd been slapped. He knew his mother was vindictive and that she could be mean when she wanted to, but this, he hadn't expected. "She managed to keep you away from us."

"Exactly. By making the judge believe I was abusive, she made sure she had full custody of you and your siblings. I wasn't allowed anywhere close to you. I didn't have a choice. I didn't have a say in how she raised you."

"Did you try?" Dorran asked. Because at this point, that was the thing he cared more about. His mother had made sure he grew up without a father, and that he never knew his father loved him. He needed to know that Angus had tried anyway, that he'd meant something to him.

"Of course I did. I was even arrested once. When things became so bad that I risked prison time, I had to back off, but I didn't stop sending you Christmas and birthday cards. I guess she never gave them to you?"

Dorran shook his head. He wasn't sure he could get one more word out. His throat felt tight, and his eyes prickled. Right now, he hated his mother.

Angus' eyes shone with unshed tears. "I'm not surprised. I knew she would take the divorce badly, but I never thought she'd push herself to that length. I never thought she'd tell you I was dead. I'm sorry, Dorran. You don't know how much. I know now that I should have stayed with her until all of you were eighteen."

Dorran took a sip of coffee because he needed to wet his throat before talking. "No, you couldn't." He couldn't imagine how staying with someone you didn't love for fifteen years would have been. He was glad his father hadn't, even though it would have changed things for him and his siblings. "Why didn't you reach out later, once we were eighteen?"

"I thought about it. I wanted to. But by that time, it had

been so long, and I thought at the very least she'd bad-mouthed me. I thought that maybe you believed her when she said I was abusive."

It made sense, but it would take Dorran a while to digest all of this. "Why now, then?"

Angus looked down. "I remarried. Fifteen years ago. I have a daughter, Rose. Your half-sister."

That was another blow. Dorran wasn't sure why, since he hadn't expected his father to live the rest of his life alone. But knowing his father was alive had been hard on him, and knowing the man was happy and with another family made things worse.

"My wife died recently. Cancer," Angus continued. "Her death made me think about you and your siblings and how I didn't want to lose you, too, not when I have the chance to have a relationship with you. I can't have anything else with her. She's gone. But you're not."

Dorran nodded. "I understand. But I'm going to need time. This is a lot to wrap my mind around, but I promise I'll think about it. I promise I won't disappear."

Angus nodded. "I suppose that's more than I can say. I disappeared from your life, and I will again if that's what you want from me. I hope it's not, though."

Dorran didn't know how to answer that.

CHAPTER SEVEN

It took more than a few days for Dorran to wrap his mind around everything. He still wasn't sure he'd done so when he met with Bettany for lunch a few days later. He'd tried getting out of it, but Bettany could be stubborn when she wanted to, and she did in this case. She'd pushed until he agreed, which was the only reason he was here right now. Well, that and lunch. He was starving.

"So, what did he tell you?" Bettany asked after taking a sip of water.

"Why do you think he told me anything?"

But she rolled her eyes. "You've never been able to hide anything, not from me. Come on. What did Angus tell you?"

"I'm pretty sure it was the same thing he told you. He asked Mom for divorce, she freaked out and accused him of being abusive. She kept him away, and he gave up."

"Did he tell you about Rose?"

Dorran nodded. "He did, and about his second wife, who died recently." Dorran had only realized he hadn't asked for details about his half-sister and his father's late wife once he got home. He'd felt like a dick, especially considering his father's second wife had died, but he hadn't wanted to contact Angus, not yet. He still wasn't ready, even though he was curious. "What do you know about them?" he asked Bettany.

Bettany leaned back in her chair. "Just what he told me."

"Which is probably more than he told me because I was a dick and I didn't ask him. I was overwhelmed."

"Yes, well, you talked face to face with him. I was on the

phone, so it was easier to push through it." She sighed. "Rose is ten. Her mother, Angela, was only forty-five when she died a few months ago."

Dorran's eyes widened. "But he's, like, sixty-seven."

"I know. I asked him about the age difference when we talked about it. He was fifty-four when they met, while she was thirty-three. The age difference is the main reason Angela's mother hates Angus."

Dorran raked a hand through his hair. "I know nothing about that."

"Well, Angela was young when she met Angus, and since her mother is only five years older than him, she was pissed. She still is. She's hated him since the beginning, and that hasn't changed. From what Angus told me, it sounds like she blames him for the illness."

"It's not like he gave her cancer because of who he was. It's not catching, and even if it was, he's not ill."

"I know that, but grief is weird."

Dorran bit his lower lip. "Do you think that's why Mom did what she did? Because she was grieving her relationship with Angus and she reacted the way she did."

Bettany snorted. "I might have believed that if she'd changed things later. She could have told us about Angus, but she didn't, and don't get me started on how she was a bitch and told people he was abusive. Look, even if she did react by instinct when he left, even if I could understand why she told the judge he was abusive, and I don't, it doesn't excuse the fact that she never told us he was alive. She could have. Even if she didn't want to tell you right away because you were so young, she could have told Chris and me, and she could have waited to explain what had happened to you."

"She did the wrong thing. I'm not debating that."

"She did more than that. She took our father from us just because he hurt her. She forced us to stay with her even though she was an alcoholic. We could have lived with Angus, and instead, we had to clean up after her and make sure she didn't hurt herself."

Dorran was surprised to hear the anger in his sister's voice. Bettany was always the one who pushed for them to take care of their mother, to clean the apartment and make sure she was as healthy as possible considering everything. She never made excuses for their mother, but she was more ready than Dorran to accept what she did. It looked like that might be in the past, though. Dorran didn't know what it would mean for the way they shared the burden of taking care of their mother, and he didn't want to think about it right now. He already had more than enough things to obsess over.

"I want to confront her."

Dorran blinked at Bettany. "What?"

Bettany pointed her fork at Dorran. "I want to confront her. I want to tell her that Angus is back and that he told us what happened, that we know she lied to us."

Dorran couldn't deny it was appealing. "You know she'll deny everything."

"She can't. You met Angus. We've both talked to him."

"She'll find an excuse, then. She'll tell us he was abusive. I mean, we only have his word that it's what happened."

"You know Mom. She's a liar."

She was. Usually, it was to hide the fact that she was drinking, although she'd gotten over that a while ago. She didn't try to hide it anymore. She was unapologetic about it because she knew Bettany and Dorran weren't going anywhere.

In the end, they decided to wait. Dorran wanted to get a better grasp on who Angus was, just in case he *had* been abusive. He didn't think so, but he had no way to know, and he wanted to be sure. Bettany wasn't happy when she left, and Dorran was exhausted.

He was grateful to arrive home finally, and even more so when Eli walked through the front door just as Dorran got a text from Carole.

"Is that from Angus?" Eli asked.

Dorran shook his head. "Carole."

"I thought you said she didn't have much to teach you anymore."

"She doesn't, but that doesn't mean we're not friends."

"That's why she's texting you? Because you're friends?"

Dorran looked at his phone. Carole was asking if he'd thought about her proposition, and he grimaced because he hadn't. He also couldn't hide it from Eli. He knew Eli wouldn't take this well, but he had to tell him. He didn't want more secrets in his life. His parents had already hidden more than enough from him. "She wants me to work with her at her shop."

Eli frowned. "As a psychic?"

Someone knocked on the door, and Dorran could have kissed them, whoever they were. He wasn't up for discussing this with Eli right now. He didn't want to think about it, even though he owed Carole an answer. He already knew what that answer would be anyway. He should probably tell her right now, but he didn't have the strength.

Eli opened the door. Whoever was in the hallway seemed to really need to talk to Dorran because the knocking was getting frantic. It was giving Dorran flashbacks of when Emanuel had been suspected of being a murderer.

It wasn't Emanuel. Instead, it was Angus and his daughter, Rose.

Angus looked freaked out. His eyes were wide, and he kept looking around the hallway as if he expected someone to jump out of the shadows. "I'm sorry. I didn't know where else to go."

Dorran briefly closed his eyes. "Come in, please."

Whatever was happening, he couldn't slam the door in his father's face, especially not with Rose there.

Dorran wasn't sure how to behave with his sister there. This was the first time they'd met, and he didn't know if Rose knew who he was. He decided that keeping his mouth shut about it was the best thing to do. Angus was her father, and he'd been the one to decide what to tell her and when.

Since it was obvious Angus wanted to talk, Dorran settled Rose in the guest bedroom, in front of his computer. He had a few games, so she probably would be busy for a while.

Eli was standing by the couch when Dorran went back to the living room, his arms crossed over his chest as he glared at Angus. Angus looked better, and Dorran sat in the armchair so he wouldn't have to take the spot next to his father. He was nowhere near ready to be that close to Angus. "What happened?"

Angus shook his head and raked a hand through his silver hair. "I'm sorry. I overreacted."

"Are you sure? Because you're here even though we haven't talked again, and even though you don't know me. You trusted me with your daughter just now."

"It's my mother-in-law. She wants to see Rose."

"And that's a problem?" Eli said. He sounded harsh, but Dorran didn't say anything about it.

"Normally, it wouldn't be, but she's been hunting me. She's hated me ever since Angela decided to marry me. She's been coming to our apartment at any time of the day and night. She doesn't take no for an answer, even when Rose has to go to school. I just needed a place where she couldn't find me for a few hours."

And he'd come to Dorran's apartment? Dorran wasn't sure he understood why, and he wasn't sure he wanted Angus to stay. The only reason he hadn't said anything about that was Rose.

"I *really* am sorry," Angus said, looking at Dorran.

Dorran believed him, but it didn't change the way he felt about this.

He was saved by another knock on the door. He and Eli looked at each other, then Eli moved toward the door. Dorran didn't recognize the woman in the hallway when Eli opened. He was grateful that Eli stayed in front of the door, his body a barrier between the woman and Dorran's apartment. "Can I help you?" he asked.

She glared at him. "I know he's here."

"Who?"

She peered around Eli, her gaze fastening on Angus, who looked like he'd seen a ghost. "Angus! Do you really think I would let you take my baby away for me?"

Angus rose from the couch. He still looked spooked, but there was a quiet strength in him. "She's not your baby, Darla. She's my daughter, and I didn't take her away from you. I came to visit Dorran and Eli. That's all."

"You knew I wanted to see her."

"You saw her yesterday. You saw her this morning. It's not like I'm keeping her away from you. But she needs more people than just you."

"And you brought her to a stranger's home? I won't allow that." Dorran wanted nothing to do with this conversation, but Darla latched onto him, maybe because he was standing close to Angus. "Who are you? Why is my granddaughter here? You're old enough to be her father." She snorted. "And Angus is old enough to be yours. You're not friends. It's not possible. What do you want from Rose?"

Dorran's back went ramrod straight at what Darla was insinuating. "I'm sorry?" he snapped.

"You have no right to my baby. I *demand* to see her."

Darla tried to step into the apartment, but Eli was there, blocking her way and forcing her back. He did so without touching her, which Dorran suspected was on purpose. Neither of them wanted Darla to have a reason to complain about him.

Her face reddened. "How dare you. You can't keep me away from my granddaughter. God only knows what you're doing in there."

Eli crossed his arms over his chest. "I would be cautious about what you're saying, lady."

"I know *exactly* what I'm saying."

"I don't think so. You just falsely accused a police detective of wanting something unsavory from a ten-year-old girl. Do you want to go down that path?"

That got Darla's attention. She took a step back and stopped trying to get past Eli. "You're a detective?"

"I am, and this is my boyfriend's apartment. If he doesn't want you inside, you're not coming in."

Her expression twisted. "Your boyfriend?"

"Yes, and before you even *think* it, the fact that we're gay doesn't mean we abuse children. Don't you dare say anything like that again."

"I didn't say that you wanted to abuse my granddaughter."

"You damn sure implied it, and you better not do it again."

Darla swallowed visibly. "I just want to see Rose. Please. Angus can't take her away from me, not after I already lost my daughter."

Dorran looked from Angus to Darla. Even though he still didn't know how to behave when he was with his father, he couldn't deny he didn't like Darla, and that in this situation, he was on his father's side. He wasn't about to step into it, though. It was none of his business, and he already had more than enough problems as it was. This was Angus' problem, not Dorran's.

"I'm not taking her away from you," Angus said again. "You saw her this morning. I already agreed that you could see her tomorrow afternoon after school. I want to spend some time with my daughter. And I know you lost Angela, but I did, too, and so did Rose. We need some time without you."

Darla bared her teeth, and Dorran knew that whatever peace they'd had for a few seconds was gone. "Time without me? Just like you and Angela had time without me?"

Angus shook his head. "How did you know where I was anyway? You followed me?"

That knocked the wind out of Darla, at least for a few moments. "Of course I did. How else was I supposed to know what you're doing with my granddaughter?"

Eli groaned. "Look, lady. I don't know what's happening here, and honestly, I don't want to know. But admitting to following Angus and his daughter around town isn't something you want to admit in front of me. You should go home. Angus said you could see Rose tomorrow afternoon. That's not too long to wait." Darla opened her mouth, but Eli shook his head. "No. You need to go. I've allowed your presence until now, but not anymore. You're insulting my boyfriend and me. You've tried to push your way into his apartment. I've had it with you, and I *will* arrest you if you continue."

If Dorran were closer to the door, he'd slam it in Darla's face just about now. But he wasn't, and Eli wouldn't do that. Instead, he waited until Darla nodded curtly, then he closed the door gently.

He sighed and turned to look at Angus and Dorran. "I have to say, I understand why you needed a safe place for a few moments," he said.

"I'm sorry about this," Angus said. "I didn't mean to bring my problems to you, but I had no idea she'd follow me."

"I don't think you could have guessed that she would." Eli rubbed his face. "I'm going to get a shower." He didn't say that Angus and Rose needed to be out of there when he came out, but Dorran wanted that to happen.

He hated that this crazy woman knew where he lived. He hated what she'd been implying even more, and he hoped he'd never see her again. He realized how vulnerable he was, being in the apartment alone all day while he worked. What was to say that she wouldn't knock on his door to yell at him again, maybe when Eli wasn't there?

"I'm sorry, Dorran," Angus said once Eli was out of sight. "I truly didn't expect this to happen. I was running from Darla, but I also wanted you and Rose to meet each other, and that didn't go as planned."

"You should probably go. I do want to get to know Rose, but now isn't the best time. What just happened made me nervous, and I don't want Rose to realize that. I don't want her to think I don't like her."

Angus gritted his teeth. "God, I hate Darla. I wish she'd died instead of Angela."

Dorran couldn't blame Angus, but he didn't want to listen to this. He didn't want a part in the situation. "I'm sorry you lost your wife and that you have to raise your daughter on your own. But please. I don't want to be involved in whatever war you have going on with your mother-in-law."

"Are you saying you want me out of your life?"

"No. I haven't made any decision about that. I told you I needed time, and I still do. I'm glad you thought about coming here when you needed a safe place, but I'm still confused." And this *Darla* thing made everything even worse. "I'm not saying I don't want you in my life. I'm only saying, give me more time."

Dorran couldn't help but think that his life would be easier without Angus and Rose in it. He suspected he would have to deal with Darla again sooner or later, and he wasn't looking forward to that. He doubted anyone would look forward to dealing with Darla. But telling Angus to leave and never come back would mean Dorran wouldn't have a relationship with him, and even though he still didn't know if he wanted one, he didn't want to lose out that possibility.

Angus nodded. "All right. I'll respect your wishes and leave. But, Dorran, please believe me when I say I didn't mean this to happen, and I want a relationship with you. With you, and with Chris and Bettany. I never wanted to leave you, and I'm sorry I waited so long to find you. I realize we won't easily become family, but I want us to work toward that goal. I don't want Rose to only have her mother's parents and me. She lost her mother. She deserves her brothers and sister."

Maybe Angus was doing it on purpose to get to Dorran, but even if he wasn't, it was working. Dorran couldn't help but think about Rose and how sad her life would be with only Angus and her grandparents in it. He didn't know what he wanted to do yet, but he couldn't ignore what would happen to Rose if he decided he didn't want his father in his life.

CHAPTER EIGHT

Sunday lunch was going well, considering everything. Dorran had arrived ready to face Eli's mother acting as if he and Eli were only best friends, and she was, but at least she hadn't asked Dorran to leave. Not that she would. If things were easier for her to deal with if she ignored the fact that Dorran and Eli were a couple, Dorran wasn't about to protest. He didn't like it, but it wasn't like he and Eli were about to have sex on the kitchen table, so it didn't matter. Eli's mother knew what was happening, even though she was trying not to think about it. Besides, the rest of Eli's family didn't seem to have a problem with Dorran's role in his life.

Everything was going decently well until Eli got a work phone call.

He got up from the table, excusing himself to answer, and leaving Dorran alone with his family. Dorran focused on his plate, and that wasn't hard to do, because Eli's mother was a great cook, and her roast chicken was to die for. But of course, this was the moment Eli's father chose to ask, "So? How are things going between you and Eli?"

Dorran didn't groan, but it was a close thing. He could have kissed Eli's brother when he said, "Dad. Why are you even asking him that?"

"Why shouldn't I? I remember I asked you how things were going between you and Andrea when you were dating."

"Maybe, but that was different."

No one said why it was different, but everyone looked at Eli's mother. Dorran quickly went back to his chicken, but not

60

before she'd realized what had happened.

She sighed. "The only reason this is different is because of me. I'm aware of that, and I'm sorry, Dorran. I'm working on it, I promise."

Dorran hated being in the spotlight like this, and he did *not* want to have this conversation, especially not over lunch and without Eli here. He couldn't ignore what Vera was telling him, though. He cleared his throat and forced himself to look at her. "It's okay. I realize it's hard for you to wrap your mind around this."

"But it shouldn't be. I know that, and I know I need to change the way I think."

"And that's hard. I'm grateful for how hard you've been trying." And he was uncomfortable and wanted this conversation to be over.

Thankfully, Eli came back. He looked worried, but that was nothing new. He always was like this when he got a call from work. It meant a new case, and since Eli worked homicides, it meant someone had died. "I have to go to work," he said.

Dorran got up from his chair way too fast, but he was glad he and Eli had come in one car. It meant Eli couldn't leave him alone with his family. Dorran loved them. He always had. That didn't mean he wasn't uncomfortable when he was with them, especially alone. The fact that most of them accepted him didn't change that. Dorran was awkward with people he didn't know well, and that meant everyone but Charlie, Carole, and Eli, and of course, Dorran's siblings. Francis didn't count, since he was dead.

Vera rose from her chair. "I'll pack you some chicken for dinner, since you didn't have the time to eat lunch properly."

Dorran knew Eli wanted to say *no* and that he probably didn't have time to waste, but he knew his mother too well. Telling her that Eli needed to go right now wouldn't change anything. If anything, it would make things worse because she'd worry Eli wasn't eating well. Then she might visit him at Dorran's place, and since he was never there, it would bring out questions he and Dorran weren't ready to answer yet. Hell, Dorran wasn't even sure where they stood.

Eli was at his place most of the time, but they hadn't talked about it, and Dorran wasn't sure he wanted to. He knew how much Eli treasured his privacy and space, even though he hadn't seemed to need it for now. He would eventually, though. They were both stubborn and had strong opinions on things, as the past had shown. Eli probably wanted to keep his private space for when he and Dorran fought. Not that they were planning to fight anytime soon, but that was life.

Dorran got up and moved closer to Eli. "Everything okay?" he asked, keeping his voice soft.

"I don't know yet."

"But someone died."

Eli sighed heavily. "Someone died," he confirmed. He wouldn't tell Dorran anything more, and Dorran knew better than to push. Besides, he didn't *want* to know.

Dorran had had enough after finding a body when he'd first moved into his apartment. The fact that he'd been involved in another two murder investigations since then didn't change anything. He didn't want anything to do with Eli's job, or with murders in general.

They said their goodbyes as soon as Vera was back with her containers. Dorran could see she was worried, but then, so was he every time Eli went to work. There was no way around the fact that Eli's job could be dangerous, but Eli was a great detective, and he was always careful. He'd promised.

"I don't know when I'll be back," Eli said as he drove Dorran home.

"That's okay. I already expected that."

"It might be later than usual, even with new cases. This case . . . it's complicated."

"It's fine, Eli. I get it. You don't have to explain."

Eli hesitated. "Your father is going to call you."

Dorran blinked. "He is?" Eli knew something Dorran didn't, but Dorran knew better than to ask questions. He wouldn't get answers, not in this case.

"I think so."

"Okay. Do you not want me to answer? Because I will, if that's what you need." Dorran was feeling better about his father's presence in his life, but he still wasn't entirely comfortable with it. It still felt weird, and he suspected it would for a while.

"I'm not going to tell you not to talk to your father."

"Of course not, but if you need me not to, I can do that." Dorran could see Eli was hesitant over this, and it made him wonder what was happening.

"Look, if he calls, it probably means he needs you. Answer, listen to what he has to say, and make your decision. I don't want to influence you."

"You won't, but you are starting to freak me out."

Eli shook his head. "You know I can't talk about it. I want to, especially in this case, but I can't."

"And that's okay. I know that."

"Talk to your father, Dorran. You'll realize what's happening when you do."

Dorran wasn't sure whether he was relieved or not that he was finally home when Eli stopped in front of his building. He was curious by nature, and he wanted to ask Eli what was going on.

Eli was right, though. Dorran's phone rang as Dorran was stepping through his front door. He wasn't surprised to see his father's name flash on the screen, and he almost dropped the phone in his haste to answer. "Angus?"

"Darla's dead."

It took Dorran a second to understand the words. "Darla?

Your Darla?"

"She wasn't my Darla."

"But she was your mother-in-law. What happened? Was it a heart attack or something?"

"I don't know. Her husband called me to tell me about it. I have no idea how it happened, though."

"What does it mean for you and Rose? Are you two okay? How did she take the news?" Dorran couldn't imagine having to tell a ten-year-old girl that her grandmother was dead only months after her mother had died. Darla might not have been a great human being, but Dorran didn't know how she'd been with Rose. Besides, Rose was a child. She had to love her grandmother.

"I haven't told her yet. Victor only just told me."

"And you decided to call me?" Not that Dorran wasn't glad Angus had thought of him when he needed to talk, but it was weird.

"Oh, I'm sorry. I probably shouldn't have, since you said you needed time."

"It's okay." Dorran suspected Angus didn't have a lot of people to talk to, now that his wife had died. He certainly hadn't been able to speak with Darla, and while Dorran hadn't met her husband, he couldn't help but wonder if he wasn't similar to her. Maybe not, since he'd called Angus to tell him what was happening, but who knew. "I do still need time, but this is a weird situation. I understand you need someone to talk to."

"Thank you, Dorran. I did. I'm not sure what this solved, but I feel better."

Dorran knew it wouldn't last. It never did, not when someone was dead.

Dorran had no idea what time it was when he jerked awake. His bedroom was dark, though, so it had to be the middle of the night. He threw his arm to the side, feeling for his cell phone, but before he could find it, the light in the bathroom went on. Dorran relaxed when he saw Eli's silhouette in the door. "What time is it?" he asked. His voice came out as a croak, and he cleared his throat.

"Sorry. I didn't mean to wake you up," Eli murmured.

"That's okay."

"To answer your question, it's going on one AM."

Dorran groaned and buried his face against his pillow. He could have done without being woken up, especially when he knew it would take him some time to fall back asleep. But since he was already awake, he might as well ask the question that had been plaguing his mind ever since Angus had called. "It's my father's mother-in-law, isn't it? The case you're working on."

Eli sighed and sat on the edge of the mattress. "It is. I can't talk about it, though."

"That's okay. I didn't expect you to tell me anything. I just wanted to confirm that you're working on that case." Dorran bit his lower lip. "And your boss didn't have anything to say about it? I mean, she kinda was family."

"Not really. She was Angus' mother-in-law, and Angus is your father, but I don't know him. He only just came back into your life, and I've seen him a few times, if even that. I've certainly never talked to him enough to get to know him."

"So it won't be a problem in case you had to arrest him."

Eli rubbed his face. "I don't know if I'm going to arrest him. I don't know if he was the one who killed his mother-in-law. Right now, I don't know anything, not for sure."

"But things aren't looking good." Dorran couldn't stop thinking about what Angus had said after Darla had followed him to Dorran's apartment. He'd said he wished Darla had died instead of her daughter. Dorran hadn't thought about that too much, because with the way Darla had behaved and the fact that Angela had been Angus' wife and his child's mother, he hadn't found that surprising. Besides, Angus had been emotional then. What he said didn't mean he'd killed her.

Eli shook his head. "Not at the moment, no. Has he told you anything? About Darla, or maybe where he was today?"

"No. He called me to tell me Darla was dead. Her husband let him know." Dorran wasn't sure he wanted the answer to his next question, but he couldn't help but ask. "Do you think he did it?"

"At this point, I have no idea."

Dorran didn't want to believe it, but he didn't know Angus. He was Dorran's father, and Dorran wanted to trust him. How could he, though? They didn't have a relationship, not yet. Maybe never, if he was the one who'd killed Darla. Dorran didn't know his father, and no matter how much he disliked it, he couldn't help but wonder. "He said he wished Darla had died instead of Angela," Dorran forced himself to say. He couldn't remember if Eli had been there when it had happened. It was probably something Eli needed to know, though.

Eli opened his arms, and Dorran launched himself between them. He wrapped himself around Eli, and Eli held him. It didn't make him feel much better, but it was something. "I wish this hadn't happened," Eli said.

"You and me both."

"I can't make you any promises. I want to, but I don't know if your father did this or not. I don't know if I'll have to arrest him. What I can tell you, though, is that things aren't looking good. It doesn't even have anything to do with what he said the other day. Honestly, I know he was overly emotional. I'm not surprised that's how he felt, considering how much he loved his wife and the fact that Darla followed him here and yelled at him. But it's obvious he and the woman didn't get along, and that means he's at least a suspect." He kissed the top of Dorran's head. "I'm sorry."

Dorran snuggled against him. "I'm sorry, too." He'd just found his father after thinking he was dead for so long. He might need time to wrap his mind around everything, but he'd thought he and his father would eventually work things out. They would never have the same relationship they would have had if Angus had stuck around, but he could have something.

Except they wouldn't if Angus had killed Darla and got arrested for it. Eli wouldn't hesitate if that was what had happened, and Dorran didn't expect him to. If Angus was guilty, he deserved to pay. Dorran might not like that, but he'd never expected Eli to turn a blind eye just because Angus was related to Dorran.

Eli kissed Dorran again. "Why don't we go to bed? I need to sleep, and you need to stop thinking about this for a bit. I'm sorry I woke you up. I tried not to."

"I'm pretty sure I would have woken up anyway. I suspected you were the one investigating Darla's death. It was too much of a coincidence that you were called out for a murder just when she died, especially when you warned me that Angus would be calling."

Dorran settled back in bed and listened to Eli move around. Eli went to the bathroom to wash up, then slipped into bed, wearing only his boxer-briefs. Dorran cuddled against him, needing the contact. He hated that he was in the middle of a murder case again, but he would do his best to stay away from the investigation. He wasn't a cop, and he didn't want to be involved.

Of course, he never wanted to be involved. Somehow, though, he always ended up in the middle of things.

CHAPTER NINE

Dorran wasn't surprised to see that Eli was already gone by the time he woke up the next morning. Things always went that way when Eli had a new case, especially during the first few days. That was when he and Mel started gathering all the information about the person who'd died and the suspects. They would have to talk to everyone, create a timeline, and everything. Dorran was mildly surprised that Eli had come home to him last night. Usually, he went home, although of course, with the fact that Angus might be a suspect, he'd probably wanted to be there for Dorran.

Dorran was grateful. He couldn't help but wonder if this was how things would be if they lived together. He wasn't about to bring that up, especially not right now with everything that was happening, but it was a thought.

Dorran rolled and snatched his phone from the nightstand. It was late, later than he would have thought, but then, he'd been woken up in the middle of the night. This was one of the things he appreciated about being freelance and working for himself. He could wake up whenever he wanted and go to bed as late as he felt like. He could start working in the middle of the day and continue until he was done. He loved having no timetable and no one to answer to.

He took his time having breakfast and showering, and when someone knocked on his door, he decided not to answer. He needed to get to work, and he knew how hard it would be for him to focus with everything that was going on.

Then Francis appeared in front of him. "You should get

that," he said.

Dorran glared at him. "I'm not planning to. I have stuff to do, and I don't want to talk to anyone." If it was important, someone would call him.

"It's your sister."

Dorran thought Francis was talking about Bettany for a moment. Then he realized Bettany would have called him before coming unless it had been an emergency. "Bettany? Is she all right?"

"I meant the other sister. Rose."

Dorran still wasn't used to having more than one sister. He supposed it would take him a while to wrap his mind around that and not think of Bettany as his only sister anymore.

"With a woman," Francis added.

Dorran would have to answer, wouldn't he? Maybe he should call Angus to ask him what the fuck was going on, but he didn't have time.

He rubbed his forehead and headed to the door. He supposed he should feel lucky he'd woken up and looked presentable. "How can I help you?" he asked when he opened. He smiled down at Rose. "I'm surprised to see you here."

The woman took the lead, while Rose stayed quiet. "Mr. Wells?" she asked.

Dorran focused on her. "I'm Dorran Wells."

"My name is Mrs. Wallace. I'm with social services."

"Social services? What's going on? What happened? Is my father okay?" Because it was the only reason Rose would be here with this lady, wasn't it?

She looked down at Rose, then back up at Dorran. "Could we talk inside?"

"Of course." Dorran stepped to the side. He hesitated, but he suspected that whatever Mrs. Wallace needed to tell him, Rose couldn't hear it. He hadn't missed the fact that Mrs. Wallace was holding a backpack that appeared full of clothes. "Do you want to go in my office and play on my computer?" he asked Rose.

She nodded, remaining as quiet as she'd been the other day. Dorran offered her his hand and was surprised when she took it, but he didn't have the time to wonder what that meant. He led her to his office and set up his computer so she wouldn't focus on what was happening in the living room.

Mrs. Wallace was still standing by the front door when Dorran went back to her. "Oh, I'm sorry. I should have asked if you wanted to sit down."

She smiled. "It's okay. I understand things are overwhelming right now."

"They are. I have to admit I'm worried about Angus."

Mrs. Wallace sat down. "You have good reasons to be. Your father is fine, physically, but he was arrested."

The bottom of Dorran's stomach dropped. "Arrested?"

"I don't have all the details, of course, but yes. The detectives in charge called me to tell me about it and that I was going to have to find a place for Rose."

"That's why you're here. Are you taking Rose to a foster family?"

"I talked to your father, and he wants you to take care of her."

Dorran blinked. "Me?"

"As far as I was able to find out, you and your siblings are his only family. I'm sure you know his wife died a few months ago of cancer."

"What about Rose's grandfather?"

"Your father told me he didn't want him to have custody of Rose. He insisted on you."

"I don't know how to deal with a child, though. Maybe you could take Rose to my sister? She has two children."

"I can certainly try contacting her, but as I said, it's not what your father wanted."

"But it doesn't make sense. I mean, Angus is indeed my father, but I didn't know that until a week ago. I thought he was dead."

Mrs. Wallace frowned. "I don't know what's happening in your life, but if you can't or won't take care of Rose, I will have to find someone else."

It would be better for Rose to stay with Bettany, but for some reason, Angus wanted Dorran to take care of her, and he couldn't find it in himself to say no.

He sighed. "She can stay here." If things got bad, he could always call Bettany and ask her for help. Besides, it wasn't like Rose was a newborn or something. She was ten, and she could probably take care of herself pretty well.

Mrs. Wallace nodded. "Good. I have a list of everything you need to know to take care of her, like her doctor's phone number and her school's timetable. She wasn't there today because her grandmother died, of course, and if I can give you advice, it would be to continue taking her to her therapist. Your father found her one, probably when her mother died, and with everything that's happening, she needs to continue talking to her."

"Of course. I won't lie. It's probably going to take me at least a few days to make sense of everything and get into a routine." And Dorran hoped his father would be out of jail by then.

"I understand, but I need you to be sure of this. I can't leave Rose here if you're not. I can call your sister or your brother."

Dorran snorted. "Chris won't take care of her. I don't think he's even met her." But then, neither had Bettany as far as he knew. But Bettany was a mother, and he knew she'd take Rose in if she had to.

"It's important for Rose to feel safe and to have a routine. I realize that with everything that's going on, it won't be easy, but you're the adult here. You're the one taking care of her, and you have to do this."

"I will." Dorran had no idea how, and he didn't know what would happen to Rose if Angus turned out to be the killer or if he was found guilty, but he didn't have to think about that right now. He should probably focus on the here and now and leave speculations to the future.

Mrs. Wallace continued to talk for what felt like hours, but Dorran barely heard anything. He knew that what she was saying was important, but his thoughts were spinning, and he needed some time to breathe, relax, and make them stop. He wouldn't be able to think otherwise.

The first thing he did after she left was reach for his phone. If Angus had been arrested, Eli and Mel had done it, since they were in charge of the investigation. He wasn't surprised Eli hadn't told him about it. He couldn't. But he was relieved when he saw a missed call on his phone. Eli had tried to call him, and whether it was to tell him what was happening before or after the arrest, it didn't matter. Even though he shouldn't, he wanted Dorran to know, and that made Dorran feel better.

God knew he needed something to make him feel better right now.

Dorran was grateful for Bettany. He didn't know how he would have gone through the day without her.

He called her as soon as he and Eli had hung up. Eli had tried calling him to tell him he'd arrested his father, and he'd been apologetic. Dorran had told him it didn't matter, and it didn't. This was Eli's job, and the fact that he'd had to arrest Angus meant he had good reasons to do that. Dorran hadn't asked, and Eli hadn't volunteered details.

So here Dorran was, alone in his living room, with his little sister sleeping in the guest room. Rose had been surprisingly tame during her nighttime routine, and Dorran wasn't sure if it was because that was how she normally behaved or because of everything that was happening. He was looking forward to getting to know her, but he wished it hadn't been this way. He also wished Bettany would have taken Rose home with her, but she already had two kids and no room in her apartment. She was ready to help any way she could if Dorran needed her, and she'd brought some clothes and toys since Dorran hadn't had the time to go to his father's apartment. He didn't know if he would be able to. It depended on whether Eli and Mel thought it was a crime scene or not.

Dorran didn't even know what had happened to Darla. She was dead, but how had it happened? If Angus had been arrested, it had to have been a murder. Dorran didn't really want details, but he wished he knew more. That was why he was waiting for Eli to come home, even though he didn't know if Eli would. He should probably have called, but he didn't feel like it. He didn't feel like doing anything but lie on the couch and stare at the ceiling.

"You know this isn't going to solve anything," Francis said.

"I don't expect it to. I just want some time to feel sorry for myself."

Francis snorted. "Well, I think you've already had more than enough time for that to happen. Eli is coming."

Dorran rolled his head to the side and glared at Francis. "You're spying on him?"

"No. I keep an eye on the front door." He wiggled his fingers and disappeared just as Dorran heard the sound of a key being pushed into the lock of his front door.

He didn't move. He stared at the door, smiling when Eli came in on tiptoes. Dorran didn't know if Eli had checked his phone. He'd been texting Eli the entire afternoon, telling him about Rose and what was happening, but Eli hadn't answered.

"I thought you'd be in bed," he said when he noticed

Dorran on the couch.

Dorran swung his legs to the side and sat up. "I don't think I'd be able to sleep even if I went to bed."

Eli grimaced. "I'm sorry."

"You don't have anything to be sorry about. You did your job, and I never expected you not to do it. I know you can't tell me anything, but I'm worried." Dorran looked toward the guest room. "I don't know what to tell her."

Eli flopped onto the couch next to Dorran. He leaned his head against the back of the couch and closed his eyes. He looked exhausted, and Dorran wanted to drag him to bed. But first, he needed to know if Eli could tell him anything.

"From what Mel and I discovered, Angus and Darla hated each other," Eli finally said, startling Dorran.

"That's not exactly a secret. I mean, he said in front of me that he wished she had died."

Eli rolled his head to look at Dorran. "You're not the only one he said that to, unfortunately. I'm not saying he's guilty because he said that. I understand how frustrated he had to have been, since I met Darla, and I know more about the situation between them now, but that's not the only thing we have against him."

"You wouldn't have arrested Angus otherwise."

"You're right. I wouldn't have."

"Can you tell me anything at all? I haven't looked in the newspapers or on the internet for details, but I can do that if you'd rather not talk to me at all."

"I'll tell you what I can. I don't like it, but I can't deny you're involved in this, and I don't want you to be alone when you find everything out." Eli straightened. "She was home alone. Victor was at the movies, apparently because she hated going to the theater. So he went alone. When he arrived home, he found the front door open. Darla was dead. I'm not going into details on her death, but she was hit repeatedly with a heavy object. Angus doesn't have an alibi. He was alone at home napping while Rose was at a play date. He had Angela's keys to her parents' house, and the murder weapon was hidden in his apartment when we searched it."

Dorran had been through enough murder investigations to know all of that didn't mean Angus was guilty. It was damning evidence, but still.

He didn't want to believe his father had done it, that he would have consciously put Rose in this situation. He loved her. Dorran was sure of that. She was all Angus had left of Angela, and he wouldn't put her at risk like that.

But the clues pointed to him. Dorran didn't doubt that Eli was keeping things from him and that he'd only given him an overview. Even that overview was damning, and Dorran didn't want to think about what else there was to the situation.

Eli reached out and rubbed the back of Dorran's neck. "I'm sorry. I wish I could have stayed out of this. I can ask my superior to give the case to someone else."

Dorran shook his head. "Don't. I trust you, a hundred percent. If you arrested Angus, I know you had a good reason to do it. I wouldn't trust anyone else but you in this situation. I know you won't stop unless there's obvious evidence and that you'll dig until you're sure Angus did it. I'm not happy you had to arrest him, but I don't doubt you know how to do your job."

Eli smiled. "Even though you had to insist for me to believe Francis had been killed?"

Dorran shrugged. "I understood why you didn't believe me. Besides, that case wasn't new." He twisted, folding one of his legs under himself so he could look Eli in the face. "I *trust* you. You know your job, and you'll make sure Angus is guilty. You arrested him for a good reason, and I won't doubt you. Just, please, give me updates? I know you can't go into details, and I don't want them. But I have no idea what to tell Rose." Dorran didn't know if she would ask, but she had to wonder where her father was and why she was staying with Dorran.

"I promise to tell you what I can. I know this is important for you. Trust me, I didn't want to arrest Angus. I wouldn't have if it hadn't been obvious. I wouldn't be doing my job if I didn't."

"But you'll continue looking into it."

"Of course I will. Mel and I will talk to Angus again, and we'll go over all the clues we have. But right now, he's the most obvious suspect, and we had to do it."

"You think I can visit him?"

Eli grimaced. "I wish you wouldn't go, but yes, of course. I understand you might want to ask him questions, and I don't know if he'll answer. He's distraught, but then, who wouldn't be? And I realize you probably have to talk to him about Rose. I have to admit I was surprised to find out he wants her to live here until this is solved."

"Since you've been investigating him, I'm sure you know he doesn't have anyone else. I asked Bettany if she could take Rose, but she doesn't have space, and she already has so much to do with two kids. She came around to help me this afternoon, but it can't be a long-term solution."

"You are."

Dorran grimaced. He and Eli had never talked about having kids, and even if they had, this certainly wasn't a great way to make that happen. Rose wasn't their daughter, and she never would be. But Dorran wouldn't abandon her. If Angus was guilty, or if he ended up in jail, Dorran would keep Rose with him. He'd raise her as well as he could, but he was terrified of what that would mean for his relationship with Eli. "I didn't want this."

Eli smiled. "But you're still going to do it. That's one of the things I love about you. You do anything for the people you care about, and you won't back down, not if it's the right thing to do. I didn't expect anything different from you."

"I know this isn't what you probably expected from our life together. I should have talked to you before accepting to take Rose in, but there wasn't time."

Eli reached out and pulled Dorran's arms. "I can't say I thought we'd ever find ourselves in this situation, but this is life. It's unexpected, and we'll have to learn to deal with it."

CHAPTER TEN

Dorran hated this place. He didn't want to be back. He *never* wanted to come back.

Yet here he was, looking at his father, both of them sitting in jail. Of course, Dorran was free to leave as soon as this conversation was over, but still. He could have done without this. He *wished* he could have.

"How is Rose?" Angus said as he slid into the seat on the other side of the glass.

Dorran was glad Rose was the first person his father asked about. It meant he cared for her. Not that Dorran had doubted that, but he still wasn't sure what to think about Angus, and all of this wasn't helping. "She's doing okay, considering. What about you? Are you?"

Angus looked around. "What do you think? I was arrested for killing my mother-in-law, even though I didn't do it."

Dorran relaxed, even though he was aware he didn't have a reason to believe Angus. "You said you wished she were dead."

"I'm sure I wasn't the only one. You met her. She didn't have the best personality, and she never made a secret of the fact that she hated me. Especially after Angela died."

Dorran tapped his fingertips on his thigh. "So you didn't do it."

Angus rubbed his face. "I know it looks bad. It's not only what I said in front of you. I was at home napping. Rose was with a friend. No one can confirm that I didn't go anywhere near Darla." He hesitated. "Your boyfriend is one of the detectives investigating this."

"No. I don't know what you're thinking, but I can imagine, and I'm not talking to Eli about this. I don't want to compromise his job. It wouldn't be fair. He's already told me much more than he should have."

Angus raised his hands. "I understand. I'm sorry I even asked. I shouldn't have. I'm grateful you're taking care of Rose."

Dorran shouldn't ask. He shouldn't stick his nose into this. Eli and Mel were working on it, and it was their job. They would find out who had killed Darla.

But Dorran couldn't help it. He wanted to believe Angus had nothing to do with the murder. "If it's not you, who?"

"I have no idea. Maybe a thief? Someone could have snuck into the house and killed her when she noticed them."

Dorran realized it was a bit of a stretch, but he wanted to believe that. "Anyone else? Maybe her husband? I mean, if she was as bad as you're saying, and I don't deny that because, as you mentioned, I met her, he might have had a motive to kill her."

Angus frowned. "I don't know. I want to believe it, obviously, but I have to say he's never struck me as a bad man."

"He doesn't have to be bad to want to kill her. I mean, it could have been a crime of passion. Maybe she made him angry, they fought, and he killed her." Dorran didn't think it had been premeditated. Eli hadn't given him details, but he had mentioned she'd been hit with a heavy object. That sounded more like she'd made someone angry, and they'd grabbed the closest thing they could find and hit her.

"Look, Dorran, I'm not a friend of his, but I don't think he would have killed her. She undoubtedly made him angry many times over the years, yet he's still married to her. He has to have his reasons, right? He has to love her. I'm telling you, it probably was a thief or something."

Dorran nodded, but he doubted that. The murder weapon had been found in Angus' apartment. That meant someone had taken it from the murder scene and had moved it there. The only reason someone would have had to do that was if they wanted Angus to take the fall for them. They had to have known how tense his relationship with Darla was and that he would make a perfect suspect for the police. No, there was more to this. Dorran could see Angus wanted to believe that theory, but he didn't. It didn't work.

"I know I'm asking a lot of you," Angus said.

"I can't say I ever thought I'd have to take care of a ten-year-old girl. It was surprising. But the social worker explained what had happened, and it was either me or social services." Although Dorran was convinced that Bettany would have taken Rose if things had come to that. She didn't have space, the time, or the energy to take care of a third child, but she'd have done it.

She wouldn't have to, though. Dorran might have no idea what he was doing, but he wasn't abandoning Rose. He didn't know what that would mean if his father was guilty but now wasn't the right moment to obsess over that. Things would work out, one way or another.

"Well, I'm grateful. I don't know how to thank you."

"Fight this. Rose needs her father, not her brother. I can take care of her temporarily, but nothing will replace you and your presence in her life."

Angus sighed. "I know. I'm not going to give up, but we both know it doesn't look good for me. I suppose I should feel lucky I won't spend too much time here either way. At my age, I doubt I'll last long if I'm found guilty."

Dorran jerked back. "Don't talk like that. You might not be young, but that doesn't mean you're going to die in here." Dorran wanted to promise he'd do everything he could so that didn't happen, but he couldn't. He didn't have a say in this. He could make all the promises he wanted, but he already knew he wouldn't be able to keep them.

"I'm trying to be realistic, Dorran. It's obvious I don't want to spend any amount of time here, but things aren't looking good. I don't have an alibi. The murder weapon was in my apartment. I have no idea how it got there. I don't have an explanation."

"You might have wanted Darla to get off your back, but killing her would have made everything harder for you."

Angus smiled sadly. "But it could have been instinct. Maybe I went there to talk to her, and we fought."

"Is that what happened?" Dorran had to ask, even though Angus had already told him he hadn't done anything.

"Of course not. I never used Angela's keys to her parents' house. I haven't even gone there since Angela died. Besides, I didn't *want* Darla to die. I wanted her to leave us alone because she's been pushing since Angela passed away, but she's still Rose's grandmother. Rose should have been able to decide whether or not she wanted a relationship with her grandparents. Now, she won't be able to."

Dorran still didn't know what to think when he left his father. He wanted to believe Angus hadn't done anything, but could he? It didn't matter that Angus was his father, or that his explanation and everything else made sense. Unless Eli and Mel found proof that pointed to someone else, Dorran didn't think this would end well. Angus couldn't prove he didn't do it. No matter how many times he professed his innocence, the only thing that would get him out of jail was proof of that.

Dorran didn't know if anyone could find that. He trusted Eli and Mel, but even they couldn't create evidence.

Dorran was relieved Rose was having a sleepover at

Bettany's home tonight. Bettany wanted her kids and Rose to become friends, and it gave Dorran some breathing room. He'd never realized how much a child could take over a life. He'd never had to think about it. But now, things were different.

Dorran needed to be careful of what he watched on TV, since Rose might hear. He needed to be careful not to swear in front of her. He needed to make dinner every evening instead of calling for takeout, because she needed healthy food and vegetables. Dorran didn't particularly enjoy cooking, and it was starting to wear on him.

Of course, that was without the Angus thing. He was in jail, and no one knew when he might be released—or if he'd ever be released at all. Eli and Mel were working overtime, which meant Dorran had barely seen Eli since Angus had been arrested. Eli was spending the night at his own apartment more often than not, now that Rose had moved in with Dorran, and Dorran wasn't sure if it was because there was now a child in their life or because he needed to keep his distance so no one would accuse him of favoring Angus.

Whatever the reason, Dorran missed him.

He flopped onto the couch and took a deep breath. It was weird to have the apartment so silent after almost a week of having Rose around. She was a quiet girl, but the TV was almost always on when she was home, and she liked to sing to herself. She hummed while she was doing homework or reading. She hummed in the car.

She'd started going to school again after Dorran had spoken to her therapist. The woman thought Rose needed routine, and Dorran was grateful. He didn't know what he would have done if the doctor had told him to keep Rose home. He'd have found something, but he was glad he didn't have to. Rose seemed to be okay with her grandmother's death, and Dorran was more than happy to avoid talking to her about it.

That was her therapist's job, not his.

All in all, Dorran's life was a mess right now, and he didn't know how to make things better. He didn't even know if he could.

The sound of the front door opening made him look up. He was surprised to see Eli step in—Eli hadn't called. "I didn't expect you to come," Dorran said. "Especially not this early."

Eli toed his shoes off and looked around. "Rose?"

"She's at Bettany's. She's spending the night there, having fun with Bettany's kids. Her nephew and niece? I guess she's their aunt, even though she's the same age as them." Dorran wrinkled his nose. That was one thing he didn't want to think about.

"Good. Wait, that's not what I meant. I'm happy to see her and to talk to her usually, but I need sleep." He rubbed his face. "I know I should have gone home, but—"

Dorran rose from the couch. "I'm glad you came here. I miss you. I know you've been going home because of Rose, but you didn't have to."

"She's already going through enough changes without having to understand why I'm here only part of the time."

Dorran frowned. "But we're together, you and me. It's serious. We could have just told her that. She doesn't have to know the details of what's going on between us, of our relationship. Besides, I doubt she cares."

"There's still the fact that I'm the one who arrested her father for her grandmother's murder. It's better like this, Dorran. Trust me."

Dorran wanted to protest, because he suspected Eli was hiding behind his professional excuse, but he did get it. Eli was trying to do his job, and he didn't want anything to mess it up. He didn't want to give anyone a reason to question the work he and Mel were doing right now.

Dorran held out a hand. "Come on. Sit down next to me for

a bit."

Eli groaned. "I really need to eat and go to bed. You know how hard I've been working on this. And that's not even counting all the other cases I'm working on right now."

"I know. I just want five minutes with you. I feel like we haven't seen each other in weeks, especially now that you've been going home in the evenings. Things would be different if you lived here, I guess."

"Maybe. I *really* need to grab a shower."

Dorran frowned. "Is everything okay? Is it the case? My father?" Or was it something more personal? They hadn't gone to Sunday lunch ever since Eli had been called to Darla's house, but Dorran knew Eli talked to his parents, especially his mother, regularly. Had she said something that was making him take a step back? Or was it really only work?

"I can't tell you about that. You know that. There's nothing new about the case, though. Mel and I are looking into it, and I promise I'll tell you as soon as we find something, even though I shouldn't. But I know how important this is for you, and for Rose."

"Okay. Thank you. I guess I was just wondering if you were overly worried about something. You don't seem particularly happy to be here."

"I'm just tired. I promise. I wouldn't be here if I didn't want to be. You know me."

It would have been easy to brush everything off, but Dorran too easily remembered what happened when he didn't push. He didn't want Eli to think he didn't trust him, but still. He had one last thing to say. "I want you to know you can talk to me. Things don't usually go well between us when you don't, like when you didn't want to tell me about your cat. You know I don't care about that, or about a lot of things. I want you to trust me."

Eli sighed heavily, and his shoulders slumped. "I'm not

hiding another pet."

"That's not what I was saying, and you know it. I realize that saying we shouldn't have secrets between us isn't realistic, especially not with your job, but when it comes to our relationship, I want you to trust me."

Dorran started to move toward the kitchen so he could put something together for when Eli was done with his shower, but Eli grabbed his wrist. "Wait. You're right. We shouldn't have secrets, not when it comes to our relationship. And this isn't exactly a secret. I've just been thinking, or anyway, I was thinking about this before this mess with your father happened. I wanted to talk to you, but then I had to arrest Angus, and I haven't been spending a lot of time with you. This doesn't feel like the right moment to do this."

"Now you're getting me worried." Dorran didn't think Eli was trying to break up with him, but he was a pessimist by nature.

Eli shook his head. "You don't have to be worried. I'm just trying to say, and I realize I am making a mess of this, that I think we should move in together. Well, I thought we should before I had to arrest your father."

"And you don't anymore?"

"I still do, but with everything that's been happening, I don't know if that's the best thing to do."

"But you still want us to move in together?" Dorran needed an answer to that. He didn't care what was happening with his father and the case, not when it came to this.

Eli smiled softly and cupped one of Dorran's cheeks. "Of course I do. I want to come home to you every night. I want to wake up next to you every morning. That's why I've been spending so much time here, Dorran. I think I'm ready for this step, and I hope you are, too."

"Of course I am." Dorran couldn't say he'd been thinking about it, but he couldn't deny he felt the same way Eli did.

He'd been in love with Eli since he was seventeen. The fact that they'd taken a multi-year pause hadn't changed that. As soon as he and Eli had met again, Dorran had started falling for him, and he didn't think he'd fall out of love with him anytime soon. He wanted them to have a life together, and moving in together was the next step.

"What about me? Are you moving in with him, Dorran?" Francis suddenly asked.

Eli jumped and pressed a hand to his chest. "Jesus," he barked out.

Dorran rolled his eyes. "I don't know, Francis. Since you've been spying on us, you know we've just started talking about it."

"I'm moving in here," Eli said, stunning Dorran.

Dorran turned his attention back to his boyfriend. "You are?"

Eli shrugged. "I don't see why not. Your apartment is better, and he's not wrong. We have to think about him."

Eli was always going to surprise Dorran, wasn't he?

CHAPTER ELEVEN

"Why are you doing that?" Charlie asked.

It took everything Dorran had not to roll his eyes. "I need silence to focus," he answered.

"Oh. Of course. Sorry."

Charlie managed to keep his mouth shut for all of one minute before asking, "Are you doing anything at all? Because it doesn't look like it."

Dorran sighed and opened his eyes. "Charlie. You wanted to be here because you were curious. You promised not to intervene."

Charlie raised his hands. "I'm sorry. I'm just curious."

"You have to admit he has a good reason to be curious," Carole said. "Besides, it's not like you need me here to do this. I don't even have to do this. I have nothing more to teach you, and you've become quite good at pushing ghosts out and keeping them away."

She was right. Even though Dorran had asked to see her, train with her, she hadn't told him anything new. That wasn't why he'd asked her to be there, though. He probably shouldn't have agreed when Charlie had wanted to be present, but he needed someone to support him when it came to this. Eli was getting better at dealing with Francis and the fact that Dorran could see and talk to ghosts, but he wasn't happy about it. Dorran didn't think he ever would be. That meant Dorran felt uncomfortable having him close any time he needed to take care of ghosts. He wanted support, and Charlie was that for him.

"Maybe," Dorran admitted. "But it still feels uncomfortable to have someone stare at you while you're trying to focus."

"He has questions. You, more than anyone, should understand that. I remember when you first realized what you could do, and you found me, and you probably had a few hundred questions you couldn't wait to ask me."

Dorran glared. "I'm not going to win this argument, am I?"

Carole shrugged. "There's nothing to win. You invited your friend to be here when you did this, and he has questions. I think it's understandable, and I'm surprised you didn't talk about this first. I mean, if my best friend could see ghosts and talk to them, I'd have a lot of questions for them right from the moment I find out."

"*You* can see ghosts and talk to them."

"You know what I mean. Now come on. Tell me why I'm here."

"To help me train?"

She rolled her eyes. "We both know that's not the correct answer. You can decide to keep it a secret if you want, but I won't be able to help you if you do."

Dorran flopped back against the couch. He was sitting on the floor, his legs crossed. That was how Carole had taught him to do this in the beginning, and while he knew he could focus just as well in any other position now, it still felt familiar to be sitting on the floor. "I need your help. I think. I'm still not a hundred percent sure I want to do this."

Carole arched a brow. "You're going to have to be more specific than that."

Dorran felt guilty about asking her to do this when he hadn't even told her he couldn't work with her, but so far, he hadn't been able to come up with a better idea. "You know what's been happening with my father," he started, unsure how to finish.

"I know he was arrested for his mother-in-law's murder."

Carole hesitated. "I haven't mentioned it, because I suspected you would rather not talk about it, but I'm sorry."

Dorran waved her words away. "I'm sorry too, and you're right, I'd rather not talk about it, but I have to. Eli and Mel are working on this, and I trust them, but so far, everything points to Angus being guilty."

Charlie snapped his fingers. "Let me guess. You don't think he is."

"I don't. I realize he doesn't have an alibi and that he had a motive to kill Darla and a way to get inside their house, but that doesn't mean he's guilty. I might not have known him for long, but he wouldn't be so stupid to bring the murder weapon back to his apartment, especially with Rose living there, too."

"You want to believe him when he says he's innocent," Carole said. Her voice was soft, and Dorran did his best to ignore the pity he could hear in it.

"Of course I want to believe him. It doesn't have anything to do with the fact that he's my father, though. I thought he was dead until a few weeks ago, and while I would be sorry if he was found guilty, it wouldn't change my life." Except for the detail that Rose would move in with him indefinitely, but Charlie and Carole didn't need to know that right now. "But I don't want to see an innocent man go to jail."

Charlie grimaced. "*That's* your problem. I understand why you think that way, but you need to stay out of it. You were shot the last time you stuck your nose into a murder investigation."

"It wasn't the last time."

"Oh, you're right. How could I forget? You were shot the first time you did that. Then you were attacked by a police officer, and remind me what happened the time after that?"

Dorran glared at Charlie. "It's not my fault I always end up in these situations."

"You could, you know, say *no*. It's dangerous. You're not a cop. You don't know how to defend yourself, as the past three times you were involved in a murder investigation have shown. You're going to get yourself killed, and I don't want to lose you, Dorran. It might be selfish of me, but you're my best friend."

Dorran knew where Charlie was coming from. He understood it. That didn't mean he could stay away.

He looked at Carole. "I want to try talking to Darla."

"Are you sure? You might not like what she has to tell you."

"I'll accept it if she says my father killed her." Although Dorran wasn't sure she wouldn't say that just because she hated Angus so much. From the claims he'd heard about the woman, he wouldn't be surprised if she did just that. "I realize I won't be able to use this to help Angus, but maybe she can give us an idea of where to look for clues. I mean, once we know who killed her, we can look at the person who did this and try to find a way to make it obvious."

"This is bad," Charlie murmured. "I'm going to be arrested. I know it."

Dorran ignored him and stayed focused on Carole. "I need you to try. Please?" Dorran wasn't sure what he'd do with the result, but he needed to be sure. He didn't know Angus well enough to be sure he didn't have anything to do with the murder, no matter how much he wanted to believe it. He might not be able to use whatever Darla would say to help Angus, and it would no doubt be frustrating that he couldn't, especially if his father was found guilty, but he had to try. He had to do *something*.

Carole nodded. "All right. What can you tell me about Darla?"

"Not much," but Dorran told her everything he knew about Darla. She listened to him, asking a few questions he answered as well as he could. Once they were done, she took her usual position on the floor next to Dorran.

Dorran had been through this more times than he remembered since he'd started training with Carole, but Charlie hadn't. He was looking at Carole with wide eyes, his mouth slightly open as she closed her eyes and focused.

There wasn't much to look at, though. She was trying to find Darla and to pull her toward Dorran's living room, but it might not work. In the meantime, she looked like she was meditating.

Dorran shouldn't have been so disappointed when nothing happened and Carole opened her eyes. "I'm sorry, Dorran. I tried, but I can't find her."

"Do you know why?" Dorran refused to believe Darla had passed on. She was the kind of person who could hold a grudge for years, and he wouldn't be surprised if she decided to haunt the ass of the person who'd killed her.

Carole's shoulders sagged. "I can only guess that is because she hasn't been gone that long. You know it becomes easier as time passes, and it's only been a few weeks, if even that. I'm sorry. We can try again the next time I see you, but I can't make promises. You know that."

"Could it be because she doesn't want to answer?"

Carole frowned. "It could be, although that doesn't happen often."

But Darla was precisely the kind of person who would do something like that. Even if Angus wasn't a killer, it would be just like her — from what Dorran knew about her — to want Angus to pay. She hated him. She might want him to pay for something he hadn't done.

Dorran checked in on Rose one last time before closing the guest room door and heading back to the living room.

Eli would be late at work today, too. He'd texted Dorran,

apologizing, but Dorran wasn't angry. How could he be? Eli believed Angus didn't have anything to do with the murder, and he was pushing to find another suspect. Or maybe he was doing it because he loved Dorran and he didn't want Dorran to lose his father. Dorran wasn't sure, and he didn't want to find out. The only thing he cared about was that Mel and Eli were working on this, spending long hours on the phone and talking to people.

Dorran was used to spending most of his time alone, but he was grateful Charlie had decided to stay for dinner. He was still spread out on the couch, idly watching TV while Dorran put Rose to bed. Dorran could see he wasn't focused on the screen, though. He wasn't surprised, not after what he, Charlie, and Carole had done that afternoon. They hadn't gotten the result Dorran had hoped they'd get, but Charlie had still been impressed, especially after Francis had used Dorran's energy to show himself.

Charlie looked up when Dorran sat into the armchair. "She's asleep?" he asked.

"She is. I'm always surprised at how easily she falls asleep as soon as she goes to bed. I wish I could do that."

"You're not ten anymore. Things are only going to get worse as you get older."

Dorran lightly kicked Charlie's shin. "Shut it. Besides, you're my age. If I get old, so do you."

Charlie straightened on the couch and turned his body toward Dorran, completely ignoring the TV now. "This is weird."

"What is? It's not the first time we've watched TV together." But Dorran knew what Charlie meant.

"It's almost like you and Eli had a kid."

"She's ten. She's not my daughter. She's my sister."

"You know what I mean. She might be your sister, but you're taking care of her. It kind of makes you a father."

"It makes me a good brother and a caretaker. That's all."

Charlie grinned. "Of course. I should have remembered you want to get married before having children. Wouldn't want them to be illegitimate."

Dorran threw a pillow at Charlie's head. "It has nothing to do with that, and you know it. This is temporary. Rose will go back to her father and their apartment as soon as Angus is released."

Dorran would miss her, though. She hadn't been here long, but it already felt like she belonged. It hadn't been hard for them to settle into a routine, and now Dorran missed her when she spent the night at Bettany's.

But she deserved to have her father, and Dorran would be more than happy to send her over to Angus as soon as he got out of jail.

Of course, that needed to happen first.

"How did Eli react when you told him Rose was going to stay with you?" Charlie asked.

"He was okay with it."

"Well, of course he was. But he's been spending a lot of time here, hasn't he? I guess I was wondering how things work with three of you. Although of course, he can just go back to his apartment if he needs privacy or whatever."

"He actually asked me if I wanted to move in with him," Dorran said. He already knew how Charlie would react, and he wasn't disappointed.

Charlie's eyes widened, and his jaw dropped to his chest. "He did?"

"Yeah. A few days ago. Rose was at Bettany's for a sleepover, and Eli came by. He spent the night."

"And he was the one who asked? Not the other way around?"

"He asked."

"I have to say I'm surprised. I fully expected you to have

to drag him to the altar or something like that."

Dorran rolled his eyes. "We're not getting married. We're just moving in together."

"Well, yeah, but I know how he feels about your resident ghost and your little ghostly gift. Besides, he's one of those guys who doesn't want to appear vulnerable."

"And living with me would make him appear vulnerable?"

"Well, not that, but asking you? Definitely. He risked a rejection. That's why I'm surprised he was the one asking. You said yes, though, right?"

"Of course I did. It's going to take a bit of time, considering everything that's happening, but we're moving in together."

"What about Francis? What does Eli think about him?"

Dorran couldn't help but smile when he remembered the way Eli had reassured Francis that he wouldn't have to leave his apartment. "He's okay with him, I guess. He doesn't act like he doesn't see him when Francis is visible anymore, and he even talked to him yesterday."

"Well, call me impressed. I didn't expect Eli to do anything like this. He cares for you, doesn't it?"

"He does." And the fact that he was ready to work through his feelings about Dorran's gifts and having a resident ghost told Dorran exactly how much.

He knew Eli didn't like this. It would have been easy for him to demand Dorran move into his apartment instead of the other way around. Of course, Francis might have been able to move along with Dorran, but Dorran suspected that wouldn't have happened. Francis cared for Dorran. They were friends. But this was *his* apartment, the place where he'd lived so many years, and the place where he had died. It had a lot of meaning to him, and Dorran was glad he wouldn't have to leave.

"Now, you just need your father to be released from jail, and everything will be peachy," Charlie said.

"You make it sound easy."

"I wish it were. Your family is so unlucky."

Dorran couldn't deny that. His brother had been accused of murdering his pregnant girlfriend and arrested even though he'd had nothing to do with it. Now his father was accused of murdering his mother-in-law, and Dorran was pretty sure he didn't have anything to do with it, either.

He expected Bettany to be arrested, too, any second now.

But one tragic situation at a time. "I don't know what it is, but I trust Eli. He'll find out who did this, and Angus will be free."

"What are you gonna do once he is? Do you still want him in your life? No offense, but he comes with a lot of baggage, especially now."

"He's still my father." Dorran still hadn't forgiven his mother for what she'd done, and he hadn't fully forgiven Angus for not trying hard enough, either. But Angus was trying now, while Dorran's mother never had. He wanted Dorran in his life, and he trusted him enough to put Rose with him when he needed to.

Charlie sighed. "I hope you know what you're doing. I mean, I want you to be happy, obviously, but at this point, I don't know how to make it happen."

"You don't have to make anything happen. I just have to hold on for a bit longer."

Charlie wrinkled his nose. "You have that much trust in Eli?"

"I do."

"Because he was the one who didn't want to believe you when you told him Francis was murdered."

"And you had to remind me of that? But yes, I trust him. Back then, I think he mostly didn't believe me because, for him, I was still the boy who'd abandoned him and had left him behind when were kids. Things are different now. He knows this is important to me, and he's doing everything he can to make sure Angus doesn't spend the rest of his life in jail. Besides, he doesn't want an innocent man to go to jail, just like I don't. It's just difficult." It was taking quite a bit of time, and Dorran knew there wasn't much time left. Eli and Mel had managed to take some time to go over the clues and everything else again, but eventually, they would have to give up if they didn't find anything new.

Dorran didn't know what he'd do if that happened, but now wasn't the time to think about it, not yet. He would have more than enough time to do that if Eli and Mel didn't find the real killer.

CHAPTER TWELVE

Dorran blinked, wondering if he'd heard that right. "You're telling me he wants to see Rose?"

Mrs. Wallace huffed. "Of course he does. She's his granddaughter."

"But he hasn't asked to see her until now."

"His wife was murdered. I'm not surprised he needed some time. But he asked to see Rose, and while you can refuse, she would do better if she had her family."

Dorran wanted to tell Mrs. Wallace Rose *was* with her family. He understood that wasn't what she was saying, though. He wasn't sure if Rose seeing her grandfather was a good idea, but he had nothing against the man. He hadn't even met him yet. He could admit he was terrified that Victor would want custody of Rose, but he already knew that wouldn't be possible for him, so it helped. "Of course. Will you be the one to organize it?"

"No." She didn't have to say that she had better things to do with her days for Dorran to understand that. It was in her tone. "If you allow me to, I'll give him your phone number. That way, you can talk to each other and make decisions together."

Dorran hesitated. His father wanted Rose to be with him, but he wasn't stupid. If Victor wanted her, he could get a lawyer and make Dorran's life difficult—more difficult than it was now. "Do you know if he wants custody?" Because Dorran had no doubt that Darla would have wanted it, if for some reason that Angus wasn't present in Rose's life.

"He didn't mention anything. You shouldn't worry too much, Mr. Wells. Even if he wants custody, I doubt any judge would give it to him. He's an older man, and he just lost his wife of several decades. He might try to cling to Rose because of what happened, but I met with him, and he didn't say anything about it."

So Dorran would have to find out on his own. *Great.* "All right. Thank you for telling me about this."

"Of course. Have you given some thought about what will happen to Rose if her father stays in jail and convicted?"

"To be honest, I'm trying to avoid thinking about it."

"I understand that, but you should. You have to make a decision about Rose's future if that happens. She can stay with you if that's what you want, but otherwise, I'll have to find a foster family." And that would give Mrs. Wallace more work than she already had.

Again, she didn't have to say it for Dorran to know that. "I'll let you know." That was the only thing he could tell her.

He hung up only for the phone to ring again seconds later. He glared at the screen and the unknown number on it. He wanted a break after the conversation he'd had with Mrs. Wallace, so he let it go to voicemail.

It rang again. Whoever it was *really* wanted to talk to him, and Dorran suspected they'd call again and again until he answered. He might as well get this out of the way. "Dorran Wells," he said when he answered.

The person on the other side of the line cleared his throat. "Mr. Wells? My name is Victor. I'm Rose's grandfather."

Well, shit. Had he been with Mrs. Wallace while she and Dorran were talking? "Of course. Mrs. Wallace called me to tell me you'd get in touch with me."

"I have no intention of taking Rose away from you. I just want to see her and make sure she's okay. What we went through . . . well, it's not something anyone should have to go through."

"I understand. I'm sure we can find a way to work together to make it so that this isn't a traumatizing experience for Rose. When did you want to come?" Dorran would have to ask Eli to be there. He didn't know Victor, but there was no way he was facing him on his own. He didn't know what the man wanted, or what he would say. Dorran needed to protect Rose, and he needed to protect himself.

"I'm outside your apartment."

Dorran frowned. "My apartment?"

"Yes. It took me a bit to find your address, but I didn't want to wait."

"But I thought Mrs. Wallace only gave you my phone number now?"

"She did," Victor answered. "Look, why don't you open the door. I just wanted to talk and see Rose."

Dorran was tempted to tell him to fuck off and come back when Dorran wanted him to. He didn't know what Victor would do if he did that, though. Would he call Mrs. Wallace to tell her Dorran wasn't cooperating? Dorran didn't know him, but he'd met Darla. If her husband was anything like her, he wouldn't trust him as far as he could throw him. "Let me ask Rose if she wants to see you."

"Of course she'll want to see me. I'm her grandfather."

"Maybe so, but like you said, the two of you have been through a lot. I wouldn't want her to be traumatized by the memories seeing you will inevitably bring back." It was an excuse, but Dorran would do whatever Rose wanted. She was old enough to make this kind of decision. Dorran wouldn't care if Victor got offended. His priority was Rose in this situation.

He hung up so he wouldn't have to listen to Victor whine about not being invited in and went to the guest room. He didn't consider it Rose's room yet, but he couldn't help but wonder if that would eventually happen. He hoped not, because she deserved to be with her father, but he couldn't deny things still weren't looking good for Angus. Eli hadn't told Dorran anything, but he was running himself ragged, trying to find proof that Angus hadn't done anything, and that was enough for Dorran to know that whatever was happening was bad.

He knocked and waited for Rose to tell him to come in before peeking his head into the bedroom. "Rose? I just got a phone call from your grandfather. He's outside, and he wants to see you."

She looked up from the book she was reading and wrinkled her nose. "Do I *have* to see him?"

Dorran stepped into the bedroom. "Of course not. You don't have to do anything you don't want to do." He paused. This wasn't something he should tell a ten-year-old girl, was it? "Well, within reason."

He smiled when that got a giggle out of Rose. She didn't smile or laugh nearly enough, which was understandable but sad. "You get to decide in this situation, though," Dorran told her. "If you say no, I'll just tell him to leave."

She hesitated. Dorran understood how hard of a decision this was. Rose had been getting used to living with him, and he'd tried talking to her about what had happened, but she'd started crying, and he'd panicked. But he thought they were making things work decently, and seeing Victor might throw a wrench into that. It might bring back memories Rose would rather not think about.

"All right. I can see him," she said.

Dorran wasn't sure whether he was relieved or not. But whatever he felt didn't matter. Rose did, and he led her to the living room, making sure she was okay before opening his front door.

Victor barely looked at Dorran. His gaze fastened on Rose

as soon as he stepped into the apartment, and he made a bee-line for her. "Oh, sweetheart. I'm so sorry," he said.

Dorran didn't intervene, but he stayed close by, just in case. It did look like Victor cared about her, though. He didn't try to hug her. Instead, he opened his arms and waited for her to take that step if she wanted to. They murmured to each other, and Dorran suspected he was asking her about him. He probably wanted to know she was safe and as happy as she could be considering the circumstances.

Dorran headed to the kitchen to make coffee, and when he looked back into the living room, Rose had left the room. Victor was still there, though, sitting on the couch and looking like someone had punched him. Dorran still didn't know if he could trust him, especially with the stunt he just pulled, but the man had lost his wife. "Everything okay?" he asked as he put the tray with the coffee pot and mugs onto the coffee table.

Victor blinked up at him. "I can't stop wondering what would have happened if I hadn't gone to the movies. Would Darla still be alive, or would both of us be dead?"

"I don't know. I don't think anyone has answers to that, and it probably won't do you any good obsessing over it." Dorran sat down and pushed the tray toward Victor.

"I was having fun while she was dying. I was watching that stupid movie, and she was probably calling for help."

Dorran didn't want to think about a murder. He might not have liked Darla, but he'd seen what human beings could do to each other. "I'm sorry for your loss." He hesitated. No matter how hard this was, Dorran needed answers. "Do you think you might want custody of Rose?"

Victor shook his head. "God, no. I love her, and I do hope I'll get to spend time with her, but I'm old, and I just lost my wife. I don't have what it takes to take care of Rose in this circumstance. But if that's okay with you, I'd like to take her out sometimes, maybe to the theater."

Dorran felt better. He smiled. "Of course. I know she wants to see the new superhero movie, although I'm not sure she can at her age."

"Oh, I already saw that one anyway. It's the one I watched the day Darla . . ." He swallowed. "I'll take Rose to watch cartoons or something. It's what we usually do."

Dorran frowned. "You already saw the new movie? Are we talking about the same one?"

Victor shrugged. "The one with the superheroes. Darla hated them, so I went alone."

Dorran slowly nodded. "I see." Except he didn't, because that movie wouldn't be out for a few more weeks.

CHAPTER THIRTEEN

Victor had done it. It was the only thing that made sense, or at least, Dorran thought so.

He knew his father was innocent, which meant someone else killed Darla. Victor had lied about the movie he'd been watching when she died. Dorran hadn't heard him wrong. He'd said he'd been watching that movie when Darla had died, and Dorran was sure it wasn't out yet. Victor might be wrong, but he had sounded convinced, and Dorran wasn't sure what to think.

Victor had been lying. That didn't mean he was the one who'd killed his wife, though. Dorran wanted to believe it was, because he wanted Angus out of jail, but he wouldn't let this cloud his judgment.

Maybe Victor had been lying for another reason. The first that came to mind was that he'd been cheating on his wife. Victor was old, but anything was possible.

And it wasn't Dorran's business. He would tell Eli about this, just in case, but he couldn't afford to try to investigate on his own. He might have, but he had Rose. He needed to keep her safe. He'd promised Angus, and that was what he would do.

He checked in on Rose, but she was already asleep. He'd made sure she brushed her teeth and took a bath, but she'd been so obviously tired. Dorran didn't know if it was the entire situation or if seeing her grandfather had touched her more than he'd expected, but whatever the reason, it was good to see her peaceful for now. He already knew it wouldn't last long. Rose was a sad child, which was entirely understandable. She'd lost her mother after a long illness, then her grandmother to murder. No one had given her details, of course, but still. The loss was impacting her, no matter how hard she worked with her therapist. Dorran wished he could do more for her, but he had no idea where to begin.

He smiled when he heard the front door open. He made sure the door to Rose's bedroom was closed, then turned to look at Eli.

He looked tired, too. He was still working long hours to solve this murder, and Dorran didn't know how to thank him. He knew Eli wasn't doing this for him or Angus but because it was the right thing to do, but still.

"Sit down," he said, pointing at the couch.

That got a smile out of Eli. "So bossy."

"You need someone to take care of you, and that someone is me. Sit down. I'll grab you some water and dinner." Dorran hadn't been sure Eli would come back, but he'd still cooked for three.

He warmed the plate in the microwave and brought it to Eli. Eli had taken off his shoes and socks and loosened his tie. He looked even more tired now that he wasn't wearing his detective uniform, as Dorran thought of it. The sight made Dorran's heart ache. He wanted Eli to be able to come here every evening and to relax. He wanted the apartment to be a safe place for Eli to let go of the day's grime and everything he had to see during the day. Dorran couldn't even imagine how hard Eli's job was. He still remembered how ill he'd felt when he'd found the body of Francis' nephew. Eli had to go through this every day.

Eli took the plate with a tired smile. "Thank you. I have good news for you."

Dorran settled next to him on the couch. "You do?"

Eli nodded, his mouth already full. "Your father will be

freed soon."

Dorran blinked. That wasn't what he'd expected to hear. "Really?"

"My boss isn't happy about it, but it was the right thing to do."

"Because you know Angus didn't do it."

"Because there were no prints on the murder weapon."

"So? That doesn't mean he didn't do it."

Eli arched a brow. "Are you playing devil's advocate here? Because I thought you'd be happy."

"I am. Of course I am. I'm just wondering if it's enough."

"It's enough for reasonable doubt, that's for sure. There was no proof in Darla's house that Angus had ever been there. The lab is still working on some samples, but everything we found came either from Darla or her husband. I'm sure the DA will argue that Angus was wearing a hat and gloves, but still. The fact that there are also no fingerprints on the murder weapon and that the killer put it in Angus' apartment also points to the fact that someone was trying to frame him. If he was smart enough not to leave physical proof behind and wore gloves, why would he have brought the murder weapon to his apartment? Especially the apartment he shares with his ten-year-old daughter."

"So you're supposed to find more proof that he did it?"

"I guess, although neither Mel nor and I think he did it, so while we're looking at everything, we're doing it with that in mind."

This was the perfect moment to tell Eli what Dorran thought of Victor. He hadn't told Eli about Victor's visit because he hadn't wanted to disturb him at work. "I got a call from Mrs. Wallace today."

"What did she want?"

"She gave Victor my phone number because he wanted to see Rose. He came by. He was already at the front door when he called to ask me if he could come."

Eli frowned and put down his plate. "And you let him in? That's dangerous, Dorran."

"I know it is. But Victor is old, and I didn't want him to tell Mrs. Wallace I was keeping Rose from him. They stayed here in the apartment, and I stuck with them the entire time. I never left them alone, I swear."

"I don't doubt that, but you shouldn't let in people you don't know."

"I wouldn't have if I'd had a choice."

"At least everything went okay."

"It did. They talked for a while, and Victor asked me if he could take Rose to the movies."

"I don't know if I'd let her be alone with him, but you're the one who has to make that decision."

"Not anymore. Angus is going to be freed."

Dorran was surprised his father hadn't called yet, but he probably hadn't had a chance yet. He was sure Angus' first instinct would be to rush to his daughter, but he had to be in bad shape after what he'd been through. Dorran needed to remember to check his phone later before going to bed.

He needed to tell Eli about this first, though.

"But something Victor said made me wonder," he said.

"Oh, God. You're doing it again."

Dorran glared at Eli. "I'm not doing anything. It's not like I was interrogating him or anything. We were having a conversation about Rose and what movie she might want to see, and I mentioned she talked about the new superhero one."

Eli grimaced. "You mean the one everyone has been talking about? Why would you want to see that?"

Dorran stuck his tongue out because he wanted to see it, too. "We're not going to talk about how much you dislike those movies. But yes, that one. As far as I know, it's the only superhero movie that's about to come out, or that's come out in the theaters recently. So I was surprised when Victor said he'd already seen it that day when Darla had been killed."

Eli leaned back against the couch. "But it's not out yet. You would have dragged me to watch it if it was already out."

"I'm going with Charlie, don't worry. I know better than to ask you to come with me when you're going to fall asleep a quarter of the way in and snore the rest of the time. But yes, you're right. The movie isn't out yet, so there's no way Victor watched it while Darla was killed. That means he lied."

"Maybe he got the movie wrong?"

"But there aren't any other superhero movies out. I also thought that he might be trying to hide something else. Maybe he was cheating on his wife?"

"I don't know." Eli took Dorran's hand and linked their fingers together. "But Mel and I are already looking into it."

Dorran was relieved. "You are?"

"Yes. Since we know Angus didn't do it, we went back to the beginning of the investigation. The husband is always the first person you look at when someone dies, and we should have dug deeper. We *would* have ordinarily."

But it had looked like an easy case, and Eli's boss had pressured him to close it and move on to the next one.

Eli sighed. "Darla had a strong personality, as you know from when she came here. From what we found out about her and her relationship with her husband, she was the same way with him. She ordered him around. I wouldn't be surprised if there was some bad blood between them." He hesitated. "Have you tried contacting her?"

"I'm surprised you're asking that."

"I wish I didn't have to. I'm going to investigate either way, of course, but it would help if we knew what she had to say."

"I tried, or rather, I asked Carole to try. She wasn't able to contact Darla, and she thinks it was because it was too soon after death. Maybe she can try again?" Dorran was stunned that Eli wanted this kind of help from him, and he wasn't about to say no.

"Please. And I'd like to be there."

Dorran wasn't surprised about that, but he wasn't sure it was a good idea. "You don't believe in this stuff."

"I didn't. Most days, I'm still not sure I believe it, but I can't deny what I've seen with my own eyes. I don't know if anything will come out of this, but I'd still like to be there."

This could either be a good thing, or a terrible one.

CHAPTER FOURTEEN

Dorran wouldn't have believed anyone who would have told him he'd be in this situation even as recently as a few weeks ago.

Gathered in his living room were Carole, but also Eli and Mel. Eli hadn't mentioned Mel would be there when they did this, and now Dorran wasn't sure it was a good idea anymore. Well, he'd never thought it was a good idea. There was nothing to lose for him, though.

"I still don't know why I'm here," Mel said. He looked confused, and Dorran got it. He knew what was happening, but even for him, it was kind of weird.

Eli's cheeks flushed. "They're going to try something."

"Okay. What are they going to try?"

"It might help with the case, to find out who killed Darla."

"You know I trust you, but I have no idea what's happening."

Eli huffed and rubbed his face. "Dorran and Carole see ghosts."

Mel blinked. "I don't know if you thought this was funny, but it's not, not really."

Dorran wished Eli had done this sooner. He didn't mind having Mel there, but he could have done without having this conversation with him. He already knew that most people didn't believe psychics or people who could see ghosts, even if they did think there was something after death. Dorran liked Mel, and he didn't want him to think he was crazy.

"It's not a joke. They really do see ghosts, and I should have told you sooner, but I didn't know how to bring it up."

Mel snorted. "Seriously? Come on, Eli. You're the last person I would have thought would believe that."

"And some days, I still can't believe I do. But I saw things. Look, why don't you sit down and let them do what I asked them to do. We can talk about this later, and you can tell me how crazy I am as many times as you want."

Dorran suspected Mel wasn't okay with this, but to his surprise, he sat on the couch instead of storming his way out of the apartment.

Dorran and Carole exchanged a glance. Dorran knew Carole didn't like working with people who didn't believe what she could do, and she wouldn't be there if she wasn't doing Dorran a favor. He mouthed *I'm sorry* at her, and she smiled and shrugged. Dorran felt even more like an ass because he still hadn't told her he wasn't planning on working with her.

"You can start," Eli said.

Dorran arched a brow at him. "Oh, thank you for your authorization. Now sit down and shut up."

Mel barked out a laugh, but he didn't say anything.

Dorran rolled his eyes and settled on the floor, mirroring Carole's position. They both had their legs crossed, and they faced each other. She nodded at Dorran, and he closed his eyes.

She would take the lead in this case, because she knew what she was doing. Dorran was only there to provide energy if she needed it to pull Darla into visibility.

There wasn't much to do until Darla got there, and Dorran forced himself to relax.

Then someone sucked in a breath, and he had to look.

Darla was there, standing by the coffee table, her arms crossed over her chest and looking like she wanted to tear Dorran and everyone else apart with her bare hands. That wasn't the most interesting thing, though. No, *that* was Mel, who was staring at Darla with wide eyes and his back pressed against the couch as if trying to get away from her.

He could see her.

From Eli's expression, *he* couldn't, though, so Carole wasn't the one doing this. Darla was only visible to those who had the gift of seeing ghosts, and apparently, Mel was one of them.

"What the fuck," Mel murmured.

Dorran wasn't sure how to help him. He needed to focus on Darla before she disappeared. Eli and Mel needed answers, and so did Angus.

"Hi," he said.

Darla turned to look at him. "What do you want?" she snapped.

"I don't know if you remember me, but—"

"Of course I remember you. You're a friend of Angus." There was so much venom in her voice when she said Angus' name that Dorran didn't doubt she hated him.

Dorran cleared his throat. "We'll let you go as soon as you tell us what happened to you. Was it Victor?"

Darla's expression twisted. "I can't believe that—that *slug* killed me. He doesn't have the balls to do something like that."

"But clearly, he did," Dorran pointed out. He was lucky Darla was dead, because he was pretty sure she would have tried to kill him otherwise.

"That dick. Where is he? I need to find him. I want to kill him."

Dorran looked at Carole. They had everything they needed. Everything they could use. It wasn't like Mel and Eli could tell anyone about this. Now they knew for sure that Victor had done it, and they could try to find proof of that. Hopefully, they would.

Angus was free, and he needed to *stay* free. He'd picked up Rose the day before, but he hadn't stayed to talk. Dorran hadn't pushed. He might not be a father, but he could imagine that Angus and Rose needed to spend some time on their own.

"Thank you, Darla," Carole said. "You can go now."

Darla opened her mouth, probably to insult Carole or tell her to fuck off, but Dorran pushed her away. He didn't want to listen to her being a bitch. She could do that in hell, or wherever she belonged.

Darla disappeared, and Mel jumped up from the couch. He rushed out into the hallway, slamming the front door shut.

Carole, Dorran, and Eli looked at each other.

Eli rubbed the back of his neck. "I have no idea what happened."

Dorran could have slapped himself for not thinking about that. "Of course. She confirmed that Victor killed her, but she didn't give us any detail."

"That's okay. Mel and I will take care of that." Eli grimaced. "As long as Mel agrees to continue talking to me, of course. I think I'm going to go check in on him."

"That's probably a good idea. Tell him that Carole and I are more than happy to talk to him if he needs to. I know how strange and life-changing this can be."

Dorran watched Eli leave. This was entirely unexpected, and he wasn't sure Mel would want his help. It might be easier for him to ignore what had happened, but Dorran had been through this. Now that Mel's gift had manifested, it wouldn't go away, no matter how hard Mel tried to ignore it. It would make his life harder unless he learned to deal with it, and to do that, he'd have to stop behaving like it wasn't a thing.

Of course, that was Dorran's experience. Maybe Mel would react differently. Dorran didn't know, but he hoped Eli would keep him up to date about it. He liked Mel, and he and Eli were best friends as well as partners. Dorran didn't want Mel to freak out and leave Eli behind, especially not now that Eli was finally starting to wrap his mind around the ghost thing.

Once Eli had left, Carole and Dorran got up. Dorran stretched out the kinks in his back and moved to help Carole gather her things, but she stopped him with a hand on his arm. "Have you thought about my job offer?" she asked.

Dorran sighed. "I have, although it hasn't been easy with everything that's been happening."

"That's okay. I don't want you to feel like I'm pressuring you, because I'm not. But like I told you, it's becoming harder to deal with the entire workload on my own, and if your answer is no, I need to start looking for someone else."

"I'm sorry, but you're right. I don't want to work with you. The only reason I asked you to teach me this stuff is that I want to be able to do what I just did and push Darla away. I don't want ghosts to take over my life, not any more than they already have. And now I know everything I need to know about that, and I hate that I can't help you with the shop, but—"

"It's not your thing. I understand, Dorran. Don't beat yourself up about this, because it doesn't matter. I would love to work with you, but I already suspected you would say no. And that's okay. I just had to try."

Dorran was glad she wasn't angry. His life was already a mess. He didn't need someone to be pissed at him, too.

"How is Mel?" Dorran asked later that day. He and Eli were on the couch, and it was weird to think that Rose wasn't in the guest room sleeping. She hadn't stayed there long, but Dorran had still gotten used to her presence in the apartment. Now that she wasn't, it felt oddly empty.

He knew he'd get over that, but he was surprised at how it

made him feel.

Eli sighed. "I'm not sure. I would say good considering everything, but it's not like I have experience in this. You and I weren't together yet when you discovered you had this gift, and I don't know what you went through. But Mel is in shock and confused, I guess. He doesn't understand what's happening."

"You told him I'd help him if he needed me?"

"I did. I don't think he'll reach out anytime soon, though. He probably needs some time to wrap his mind around things and to ignore it."

"As long as he knows he won't be able to do that forever. You know how that went for me."

"I do. Maybe I can give him Carole's number? I don't know if he'd rather train with you or with her, but that way, he'll have an option." Eli hesitated. "You talked to her while I was outside with Mel, didn't you?"

"I did."

"Are you going to take the job?"

Right. Dorran had mentioned it to Eli, but they hadn't had a chance to talk about it. It had slipped his mind, and clearly, the same had happened to Eli. He hadn't forgotten, though. Dorran was surprised he wasn't angry at the job offer. There was no way he was happy about this, and he'd probably try to dissuade Dorran if he accepted the job, but he wasn't reacting the way Dorran expected him to.

Dorran didn't want him to work himself up for nothing, though. "I told her I couldn't do it."

Eli squeezed Dorran's hand, and Dorran snuggled closer to him. He knew Eli was glad for that, so he was surprised yet again when Eli said, "You can say *yes* if that's what you want."

Dorran tilted his head up to look at Eli. "You don't want me to do it."

114

"You're right. I don't. I might believe you have this gift now, but you saw how Mel reacted, and he saw Darla's ghost with his own two eyes. The people I work with are going to find the fact that my boyfriend is a psychic hilarious. But you are the one with this gift. I don't have it, and I don't have a say in this decision. I don't know how it works or what it feels like. But I trust you to do the right thing."

Dorran beamed. He and Eli had come a long way. They'd gone from disliking each other after all those years they'd been apart to being a couple and Eli accepting what he could do. Well, accepting it might not be the best word for it, but he wasn't running away, and he'd admitted Dorran had the gift. He wasn't ignoring it anymore. He didn't like it, but he was working on that. "I don't want the job."

"Are you sure? Because like I said—"

"I'm sure. I never wanted to learn this because I wanted to use it. I just wanted to be safe from ghosts. I want to be able to keep them away from me."

"Except Francis."

"Well, Francis isn't going anywhere. Besides, I kind of like him."

Eli chuckled. "Only kind of? You would have kicked out any other ghost from the apartment. Admit it. You like Francis. He's your friend."

"You're right, he is. I don't want him to leave. I know you're not comfortable with him around, but this is his home."

Eli shook his head. "I don't want him to leave, either. You're right. This is his home. I won't deny it makes me uncomfortable, and I could do without him looking at us when we have sex, but I've accepted the two of you are a package deal. That's why I want to move in with you rather than the other way around. I know you don't want to leave Francis behind. I can't say I'm comfortable with his presence, but I know we can make things work. I'm ready to compromise for that to happen. I don't want to lose you."

Dorran hooked a hand around Eli's neck and pulled him down to kiss him. "You won't lose me. We've had our ups and downs, and that will continue happening. It's life, and you and I have never done things the easy way. But I'm not giving up on us. I hope you'll never ask me to choose between you and Francis, or Charlie or my father, because I don't want to make that choice."

"I won't ask that of you."

"Good. That means we're already compromising. See? We can make this work."

Eli poked Dorran in the side. "You'll have to talk to Francis, though. I don't mind having him live here with us, but he needs to stay out of the bedroom."

"I promise I'll talk to him."

"That's all I want."

Dorran was done talking. He swung his body up and around, straddling Eli's lap. Eli cupped Dorran's ass with both hands and pulled him closer, but he stopped short of kissing Dorran. He looked around, then back at Dorran. "Is he here?"

Dorran laughed. Life was never going to be boring, between Eli and Francis, and Angus and Rose. Dorran still didn't know if Angus would make it out of this or if he'd have to go back to jail, but he didn't want to think about that right now.

Right now, he wanted to focus on Eli.

"I don't know, and I'm not going to try to get him to show himself. That'll only get his attention, and then he *will* stick around to watch."

Eli's hands tightened on Dorran's ass. "And there will be something to watch?"

"Yes, please," Francis said from somewhere behind

Dorran.

Dorran grabbed one of the couch pillows and threw it without looking. Even if he nailed Francis' position, the man was a ghost. The pillow wouldn't touch him.

"That's not fair!" Francis cried out. "You're in the living room. Where am I supposed to go? In the guest room bathroom?"

"Wherever isn't here," Dorran answered, but Eli was already getting up and pushing Dorran off his lap, grabbing him and dragging him to the bedroom. Dorran laughed, not angry at Francis and delighted at Eli's reaction. He hadn't ignored Francis or demanded he leave. Instead, he behaved as if Francis were a housemate, as if he belonged in the apartment as much as Dorran — and now Eli — did.

The door had barely closed behind them when Eli was throwing Dorran onto the bed. He stood there for a moment, looking at Dorran, and Dorran decided he needed to do everything he could to get to the point. He loved when they took things slow, but his heart felt like it might burst with love for Eli, and he needed Eli inside him.

He rolled to his front and snagged the lube from the nightstand drawer. He laughed when Eli grabbed his feet and pulled until his legs dropped off the bed. His eyes widened when instead of turning him around, Eli pushed down his soft pajama pants — and the underwear Dorran wore underneath. Warm hands palmed Dorran's ass cheeks, and he twisted his arm back to hand Eli the lube. He had no idea what Eli had in mind, but he was grateful he'd taken a shower an hour ago, and that dinner had been light.

He shivered when he felt the first touch of Eli's slick tongue on his hole. This wasn't something they did often. They had sex almost every time they shared a bed, but it was mostly blowjobs and handjobs, maybe frotting if they felt particularly frantic.

Eli was anything but right now.

He took his time, mapping Dorran's ass with his tongue and lips, drawing invisible signs on his skin with his fingers as he held him open. It was an incredibly vulnerable position, but aside from a slight embarrassment, Dorran felt okay.

More than okay.

He felt like he might come any second by the time Eli finally pushed a finger inside him and asked, "Do you want to move up the bed?"

Dorran didn't think his knees would hold him up if he tried moving, so he shook his head. Eli leaned over him, pressing his chest against Dorran's back, and gosh, they were still mostly dressed, and it shouldn't have been so hot. "You sure? The floor can't be comfortable for your knees," Eli said.

Dorran glared at the comforter. "Just fuck me." Dorran felt vulnerable, but he wanted to be with Eli. He wanted Eli to have all of him, to protect him, to fill him, and never let him go.

Thankfully, Eli didn't ask Dorran if he was sure again. Instead, he pushed another finger into Dorran's ass, and what felt like *decades* later, finally took his fingers out to replace them with his cock. Dorran whined when Eli entered him. He wasn't in pain except for his blue balls, and he needed to come *now*. Luckily for him, he didn't have to ask. Eli seemed to understand what he needed, and he pushed inside him, hot and smooth, opening him up and never stopping as he started fucking him. His movements were sure and hard, and he held Dorran by the hips as he hammered into him. Dorran's cock rubbed against the comforter, giving him all the contact he needed on his cock.

Dorran wailed—a sound that he couldn't believe came out of him—and came all over the comforter under him. It seemed to spur Eli on, because he slammed his hips against Dorran's ass, pressing and pushing and fucking him until

Dorran's knees trembled, and Eli filled his ass.

Eli flopped onto Dorran, burying his face against the back of Dorran's neck, lightly biting him there and making him shiver again. Dorran's knees ached, his legs were stiff, but he'd never felt so good. "Do you think Francis spied on us?" he asked. He wouldn't put it past the ghost.

Eli chuckled. "Well, we sure gave him a show."

CHAPTER FIFTEEN

"How are you doing?" Dorran asked Angus.

Angus and Rose had come around today. Rose seemed happier, but she was still as quiet as she'd been when she lived with Dorran. She told him she'd missed him, though, and that had made something warm in him. They were siblings, but she was so young, and they barely knew each other. Dorran had been terrified of what being in her life might be like, but they'd lived together, and everything had been okay. Not great, considering the circumstances, but good enough.

Still, he was grateful he wasn't in charge of her anymore.

Angus sighed and leaned against the couch. "I've been better, but I'm glad to be out of there."

"I bet. Have you talked to Bettany and Chris yet?"

Angus grimaced. "I called Bettany, and she was happy to hear from me. But I have no way to contact Chris. I don't think he wants to talk to me."

"Well, he was seventeen when you left. He felt betrayed, and he still does. I guess things were easier for me because I was so small when it happened, and I can't remember a previous relationship with you. He can, and after everything he's been through, I think he doesn't want to lose someone else." It was a pity, because they shared an experience. They'd both been imprisoned for a murder they hadn't committed. They'd both lost someone they loved, albeit not in the same way.

Angus rubbed his face. "I wish I'd pushed more. I wish I'd never left. Things would have been different if I'd stayed with Regina."

"You can't think that way. You couldn't have imagined she'd do something like what she did. You thought you were doing the right thing, and while you made mistakes, you're trying to fix them. Chris will see that eventually. Give him time."

Angus looked toward the guest room. Rose was in there right now, playing on Dorran's computer. This wasn't a conversation to have with a ten-year-old kid in the room, and Dorran suspected Angus needed some adult time to talk through his experience. It was obvious he worried about her, though.

"She'll be okay," Dorran told him.

"I hope so. I'm doing my best, but I can't help but wonder if that's enough. I don't know how to be a father. I wasn't to you."

"Because you never had the opportunity to do it. But you've been with Rose since she was born, and you're a good father. I can see that in the way you behave with her. I'm not going to say she's okay, because I don't think she is, not after everything she's been through. But you're there for her. You're making sure she eats, that she goes to school and that she sees her therapist. There's nothing else you can do but love her."

A knock on the door interrupted them. Dorran didn't mind—he wasn't great at important conversations like this one. He never knew what to say or how to help. He wasn't a father, and he'd never been incarcerated. He'd never been accused of something he hadn't done. He didn't share those experiences with his father, but he wasn't sure that anything he could say would help.

He patted Angus' knee and rose to answer. He thought it might be Emanuel, who was the only one who visited without warning Dorran first and didn't have a key.

It wasn't.

Victor stood in the hallway, his face a mask of anger. Dorran took an instinctive step back. He knew Victor was a killer, even though Eli and Mel hadn't yet managed to find proof of that. They would, eventually, but Dorran didn't want to talk to the man before it happened, or ever again. "What do you want?" he asked. He'd probably be better off slamming the door in Victor's face, but he couldn't know how Victor would react to that. He might be an older man, but that didn't mean he was harmless.

"He's here, isn't he? I went to his apartment, but he wasn't there."

"That's none of your business. Leave him alone." Victor had already killed his wife. Dorran didn't want to risk him hurting Angus.

Victor pushed past Dorran. Dorran hesitated, not wanting to hurt him by pushing him away, but by the time he decided he would risk it, it was too late. Victor was in his apartment, facing his father — and brandishing a gun.

Dorran's breath hitched. He hadn't seen the gun earlier, and he prayed Victor wouldn't use it.

"You killed her," Victor yelled. "You should be in jail. Instead, you're free, and the police are interrogating me."

Dorran needed to redirect Victor's anger. It was probably stupid, but it was the only thing he could think about right now. "But you killed her."

That did the trick. Victor spun on his heels and looked at Dorran. "What did you say?"

Dorran crossed his arms over his chest. "That you killed her. That's why the police are interrogating you, isn't it? My father is innocent, but you're not. They already know it. They just need proof."

"Dorran," Angus murmured, but Dorran ignored him. He couldn't allow himself to be distracted.

Victor's expression twisted. "You would have killed her

too if you had to live with her for thirty years," he spat out.

There it was. Victor had confessed, and while Dorran wasn't sure if it would be enough for Mel and Eli or for a jury to convict him, at least Victor wasn't trying to blame Angus anymore.

"This is my chance to be at peace finally," Victor continued. "I won't let you or anyone else ruin it. I deserve to be alone. I deserve to be free."

Dorran didn't know what to do. He couldn't call Eli. He couldn't let Victor continue what he was doing, because Rose was in the guest room. It was a miracle she hadn't come out yet. Dorran had to find a way to get Victor to drop the gun, and he had no idea how to do that.

He focused on Darla. He didn't know if this was going to work, if he had enough energy in him for her to take and use to appear in front of Victor, but it was the only thing he could think about. He needed to distract Victor for long enough that he could somehow take the gun away from him.

He was probably about to get shot again, but there was nothing else he could think to do.

Dorran knew the exact moment Victor noticed her. He didn't know if Angus could see her, but since his eyes had gone wide, he probably could. Keeping her here, keeping her visible, was making Dorran tire quickly, but he had to push through.

"You," Darla said. She didn't even glance at Angus, even though she'd hated him when she was alive. No, all her attention was on Victor. "You killed me."

Victor had gone pale, so much that Dorran wondered if he was about to faint. He wouldn't be surprised if that happened, but he didn't want the gun to fall and to go off.

Angus reacted before Dorran could, reaching out and grabbing the gun from Victor's hands. Victor scrambled to take it back, but even though both men were older than Dorran,

Angus was taller and better built. He was stronger, and he managed to keep the gun away from Victor. The fact that Darla was screaming at Victor that he was an asshole and that he needed to rot in hell for killing her probably wasn't helping Victor.

Dorran resisted the urge to punch Victor in the face and abandon him to Darla's yelling. He took his phone and called Eli, quickly explaining what was happening. Something needed to be done, and fast. Angus was still holding the gun, and Rose was in the guest room.

"Dorran?" Angus asked, his voice quiet, probably so that Victor wouldn't notice him.

"I don't have a safe for you to put that in. You need to keep it out of reach from him. Maybe on top of the kitchen cupboards? I already called Eli, and he and Mel are coming." Victor wouldn't be able to reach up there, even if he managed to stop looking at Darla for a bit.

Angus nodded and reached up. He had to stand on his tiptoes to reach above the cupboards, but he managed and slid the gun there.

Then he turned to Dorran. "What is happening?"

Dorran shook his head. "Not now." Not ever, if he had a choice. He didn't want to explain to Angus that he could see ghosts. He'd probably have to, though. He didn't know if it was a coincidence or genetic, and if there was even one chance that Rose was like him, he wanted Angus to know. But Bettany and Chris didn't have this ability, not as far as Dorran knew, but better safe than sorry.

"I don't need to go to the hospital," Angus snapped at the woman who was trying to convince him to go with her.

Dorran wasn't sure why Eli had called the EMTs, although he supposed it was, in part, his fault. He should have been clearer when he'd told Eli that Victor was in his apartment with a gun threatening him and Angus. He hadn't taken the time to explain the rest of the situation, and this was the result. Eli had freaked out that Dorran might be hurt, and he called the EMTs, who were now trying to convince Angus to go to the hospital since Dorran had told them that Angus was the one who'd taken the gun from Victor.

"No shots were fired," Dorran said.

"You heard him. He was here, too. Why doesn't he have to go to the hospital while I do?" Angus asked.

Dorran glared at him. "This is how you thank me for trying to help you?"

Eli cleared his throat. "Can we go back to what happened?"

He'd relaxed when he'd seen that Angus and Dorran were okay. He and Mel had busted through the front door, guns ready, and they'd found Victor still staring at the corner of the room. Dorran suspected Mel could see Darla still yelling, but he had ignored her as he and Eli made a beeline for Victor and arrested him.

"We already told you. Victor came in, yelling that it wasn't fair that Angus had been released and that he was being interrogated instead of Angus."

"And then?"

Dorran wasn't sure how to answer that. He could tell Eli what had actually happened, but there was no way Eli could write it down for anyone to see. Dorran doubted that *Victor saw his dead wife's ghost and freaked out* would be accepted by anyone as the reason Victor had allowed Angus to take the gun from him. "I'm not sure. I mean, Victor is kind of old. Maybe he wasn't feeling well. My father managed to grab the gun from him while I distracted him by telling him I thought he'd killed his wife. Victor didn't fight back. I think he realized that whatever happened, he'd done this, and nothing would change that. Maybe he didn't want to make things harder by trying to hurt us, especially with his granddaughter in the other room."

Eli's expression told Dorran he was aware there was more to it and that they'd talk about it later. That was fine with Dorran. Eli needed to know the truth, but right now, he wanted everyone to leave his apartment.

He needed some space to breathe and relax. He'd had enough of being shot at, being threatened with guns, being involved in murder investigations.

He knew it wasn't Angus' fault. He might have hated Darla, and he might have wished her dead, but wasn't that normal? Dorran had met Darla, both when she'd been alive and after she died. She hadn't been a pleasant woman, and he could understand how she'd pushed Angus to the point that he wanted her dead.

But he hadn't killed her. Her husband had, and now he would pay for it. Dorran was satisfied, even though he wished he hadn't been involved in this.

"We really need to check you, sir," the EMT told Angus. "You're a certain age, and we have to make sure your heart and everything else is in order after what happened. It was a very stressful situation."

"I can't leave my daughter alone," Angus said.

Dorran knew his father wasn't hurt, but the EMT was right. He was almost seventy, and he'd been through a lot, between jail and what had just happened. Dorran would feel better if a doctor checked Angus out and reassured him everything was okay. "I'll take care of Rose," he said. "We'll follow you to the hospital. I promise I'll do everything I can to keep her calm and to explain that you're okay and that the doctor wants to make sure of that."

"Are you sure? I've already asked so much of you."

"We're family. I want to be sure you're okay."

That finally got Angus to agree.

Dorran was relieved.

"All right. I'll see you there?"

"You will. I'll explain what's happening to Rose, and I'll take her to Bettany. That way she can spend some time with Bettany's kids. I think that will be better than having to be in the hospital. Who knows how long it's going to take?"

"That's a good idea," Angus agreed. "Thank you. I know you don't have to do this, but I'm grateful you are."

"Don't even mention it. I told you, we're family. We might be dysfunctional, but it doesn't mean we don't care for each other." Dorran hadn't been sure he wanted Angus in his life after Angus had first reappeared, but he was now.

No matter what had happened in the past, it had been almost thirty years. Angus wasn't the same man he'd been then. He was trying, and that was the important thing. Dorran didn't want to lose him. He almost had, and that made him realize that he didn't care about what had gone down when he was three. He cared about what Angus was doing now, and it was obvious he loved Rose and that he wanted the best for her.

That was what Dorran told Angus once he joined him at the hospital. He wasn't surprised to see Angus was alone in his hospital bed, people walking and talking around him. Angus looked stubborn, which was something they had in common. Dorran was ready to bet his father would run away as soon as he had the opportunity. He didn't like hospitals, although who did?

"Are you okay?" Dorran asked as he settled in the hard, plastic chair next to the bed.

"They want me to stay overnight," Angus grumbled.

"Well, you've been through a trauma."

"I think the worst part was seeing Darla again, especially knowing she was dead. I thought I was finally free of her."

Dorran rolled his eyes. "That's the kind of thing that got you arrested in the first place."

"But she's dead, Dorran. How is that possible? You saw her, didn't you?"

"I did." Dorran took a deep breath. "I have something to tell you. Well, more than something."

Angus frowned. "I'm listening."

"The first thing is that I want this to work. I want to be in your life and Rose's. I want us to try having the kind of relationship we should have, considering you're my father."

"That's great. Thank you for giving me this chance."

Dorran raised a hand. "But you need to know everything before you agree to this. Some time ago, when I first moved into my apartment, I found a body. I've been involved in several other investigations since then, but it wasn't on purpose. The reason is that I can see ghosts."

Dorran was afraid to look at Angus. He'd been lucky Eli hadn't rejected him when he'd found out what Dorran could do. Neither had Charlie, and they were the only two who knew. Dorran hadn't yet dared tell Chris and Bettany, but he would, eventually. The thought was petrifying, though.

"So what? You're psychic?"

"I don't know if that's what I call myself, but I guess. I see ghosts, and I can talk to them. I can push them away if I don't want them to be there, and in some cases, like today, I can make some of them come to me and make them visible to everyone."

Understanding dawned on Angus' face. "That's why Victor and I saw Darla."

"It is. I needed to distract Victor, and I wasn't sure how. I forced Darla to appear."

"It was the right decision. You managed to distract him, and I got the gun from him. Things could have gone much worse. It was quick thinking, Dorran, and it was the right thing to do."

Dorran blinked. That wasn't what he'd expected when

he'd thought about telling Angus about this. "You're taking this well."

Angus shrugged. "It's not the first time I've heard of that kind of thing. I don't have the kind of ability you have, but my grandmother did. My mother didn't believe it, but my grandmother told me about it. She wanted me to know if I happened to have the ability." He sighed. "Dammit. This is one more reason I should have stuck around instead of leaving. It had to have been terrifying for you to find out about this."

"I guess I'm lucky it didn't happen until recently. I don't know how I would have reacted if I'd been a kid. But I wasn't, and I'm fine. I had help from a psychic, and she told me how to push the ghosts away and make sure they didn't take over my life. I'm okay. It was a surprise, but it's something I can deal with."

Dorran hadn't been sure about that in the beginning, but he was now. He might never want to use his ability to make money the way Carole did, and he might be selfish for not being willing to help families talk to their loved ones, but that wasn't his life. This was, and he didn't want it to change.

Well, he didn't want it to change any more than it already had recently. Dorran was done with changes. He had everything he could want — his family, his job, his apartment, and Eli.

CHAPTER SIXTEEN

Dorran wasn't sure he was doing the right thing, but he felt like he had to do this.

He could do without confronting his mother about what had happened with his father. He already knew the story, and none of that had impacted his newfound relationship with Angus. He didn't need any more answers. He didn't need to know why his mother had done what she'd done.

But he wanted to know anyway.

He knew what had happened, but he still had a hard time believing his mother could have done what she'd done. She was an alcoholic. She could be mean. She didn't seem to care about Dorran and his siblings most days. But this was so much more than that.

She'd taken Angus' children away from him, knowing exactly what she was doing. That had been her revenge. He'd left her because things weren't working. He might have broken her heart, but that wasn't a good enough reason to do what she'd done. She'd lied to a judge. She'd lied to everyone. What if Angus had been arrested for his supposed abuse?

That was why Dorran was here. He stood in front of his mother's front door, wondering if he'd get the answers he wanted. He already knew this wouldn't end well, but he had to try.

He didn't knock. He never did. "Mom?" he called out as he stepped into the apartment.

She didn't answer, but he knew where to find her. Sure enough, she was in her armchair, an almost empty bottle on the table next to it. For once, Dorran ignored it. He ignored the mess in the room—his instinct was to clean up and make sure she was okay.

He still cared about her, even though he didn't want to, even though it didn't make sense. After everything she'd done, he should hate her. But he'd stopped feeling anything for her a long time ago, except maybe pity and that lingering sense of love he had for her because she was his mother. He was responsible for her.

That was it.

Dorran crouched in front of the armchair. He put a hand on his mother's knee and shook it until she opened her eyes. "Come on. I need to talk to you," he said.

She groaned. "Dorran? What you want?"

"I want to know why you told everyone my father abused you. I want to know why you said he was a danger to me, Chris, and Bettany. I already know why you told us he was dead, and I wasn't surprised to find out that wasn't the worst sin. You lied. You intentionally kept him away from us. You took our father away from us, and I will never forgive you for that."

She blinked. "Your father?"

"He's back. He contacted me a few weeks ago." That was all she needed to know. Dorran wasn't about to tell her about Angus' mother-in-law and what had happened. His mother would no doubt try to convince him that his father had killed Darla, and he didn't want to have to listen to that. He already knew the truth.

His mother tried to sit up, but she didn't seem to be able to coordinate her limbs. One of her hands slipped, and she slumped back into the armchair. "Angus?" she asked.

Dorran shouldn't have come here when she was drunk, but then again, she was never sober. "He contacted me a few weeks ago," Dorran repeated. "That's why Chris, Bettany, and I came to talk to you. He told us what happened thirty years ago. He told us what you did."

She shook her head. "You can't trust him. I trusted him, and you saw how that went. He abandoned me." A tear rolled down her cheek, and Dorran wasn't sure it was real or not.

"He divorced you. Things weren't working, and he didn't want his life to be ruined."

"He abandoned us!"

Dorran jerked back. "He left *you*. The only reason he didn't come back is that you made sure he couldn't. You lied about him. You lied to us. Why did you do it? Was wanting a divorce really that bad? People divorce every day. They build new lives and are happy even after that."

"He was going to leave me alone. He was going to take you. I know he was. I couldn't let that happen."

"You didn't want to lose me?" Dorran was surprised to hear that. His mother hadn't been drinking as much when he was growing up as she did now, but she'd been distant. Bettany had been more of a mother to Dorran than his actual mother had.

"I didn't want to lose him. It wasn't right. He didn't have a reason to leave me."

"But he did."

She smirked. "He did, and he paid for it."

"You're not even sorry, are you?" Dorran already knew the answer to that. It was obvious on her face. She might be crying, and she might even be sorry about what had happened, but it wasn't for what she'd done.

She still resented Angus, and she probably always would.

Dorran got to his feet. He hadn't needed these answers, but he was glad he had them. His mother had never felt sorry for what she'd done. She still didn't. She was still living in the past, and Dorran pitied her for that. To his surprise, he wasn't angry. He'd already known how this would go, and he'd been prepared.

Years had passed, and Dorran didn't want to live in the past like his mother was doing. That wouldn't end well.

Dorran didn't feel sorry when he left his mother to her tears and her bottles. He knew he would be back eventually. He always was. No matter what he felt about her, he was responsible for her. If he and Bettany didn't take care of her, no one would, and she'd eventually die. Dorran didn't want to be responsible for that. He didn't deserve to feel guilty about it for the rest of his life.

His phone rang as he stepped out of the building and took a deep breath of fresh air. He smiled when he saw it was Eli. Eli was worried about him, now more than ever. Dorran wasn't stepping in front of bullets this time, but he'd faced a lot of emotional turmoil, and Eli cared. He wanted Dorran to be happy, but there was nothing he could do to make that happen, not in this situation.

"Hello," Dorran answered.

"Are you okay? Are you still at your mother's?"

"I just left."

"Did you get the answers you wanted?"

Eli hadn't thought this was a good idea, and maybe he was right. Talking to his mother hadn't brought Dorran closure or anything like that. "I did. She didn't deny what she did, and I'm sure she did it because she wanted revenge. I don't know why she was so keen on having Angus in her life, and honestly, I don't care. Maybe she didn't want to be alone. But she had no right to do what she did, and I don't know if I can forgive her for that."

"But you'll continue taking care of her, won't you?"

Dorran smiled. "How do you know?"

"That's how you are. No matter how you feel about her, you won't abandon her. It's one of the reasons I love you."

"One of the reasons?"

Eli chuckled. "Now you're fishing for compliments." He sighed. "I have to go back to work. I just wanted to check in on you."

"Don't worry about me. I promise I'm fine. This was exactly the way I expected it to go, and I was ready for it. Now get back to work, finish as soon as you can, and come home."

Dorran knew things wouldn't be easy. He had no idea how to deal with his father, and even though Angus wasn't trying to parent him, it was still a strange relationship. He knew even less how to deal with Rose, but he supposed he'd learn, just like he'd learned to deal with his mother as he grew up. At least Rose was more pleasant to be with.

Dorran couldn't have imagined this was how his life would be when he'd found the body of Francis' nephew, and some days, he still couldn't believe it. He had a boyfriend, he'd made peace with his brother, and he'd gotten back the father he thought was dead.

His life was aligning, and if he played his cards right, he'd be happier than he'd ever imagined.

EPILOGUE

"How many boxes are still downstairs?" Dorran asked. He felt like he'd climbed the stairs a hundred times rather than going up and down the elevators with Eli's boxes. How on earth had Eli managed to accumulate so much stuff? And they weren't even moving the things Dorran already had, for example, the stuff in the kitchen and most of the furniture.

"I saw five," Mel said. He exited the elevator carrying a box and headed inside the apartment.

"We need to hurry. I still have to finish the cooking."

"Not my problem if you decided to invite Eli's family over for Sunday lunch on the day he was moving in," Mel called back.

In hindsight, that probably wasn't one of Dorran's smartest ideas.

Eli had decided to move on a Sunday because the probability that he'd be home that day was much greater. He could have taken a day off work, but they were planning to take a week off and go somewhere, and he wanted to keep his days for then. Dorran needed some time away from the city and the mess that his life was.

It was a good mess, a mess made of people and love and family, but Dorran wasn't used to it. Once, he'd only had his mother and Bettany, and Charlie when he could bring himself to step away from Theresa. But now there was so much more. There was Chris and Angus, and of course, Rose. There was Eli's family and Mel. It was a lot of people for someone who was used to being on his own.

And Dorran had probably made things worse by inviting Eli's family over for lunch.

The apartment was still full of boxes. Eli's cat was hiding under the bed and showed no signs of wanting to ever come out. Dorran had decided to cook lasagna because it was fairly easy and wouldn't require a lot of clean up, but he was still overwhelmed.

He grabbed the last box from the elevator and allowed the door to close. It immediately went down again, probably called by Eli, who needed to fill it with his last boxes. Dorran carried the box into the apartment, ignoring Francis, who was leaning against the doorframe and smirking. He knew Mel had ignored the ghost, too. So far, Mel hadn't wanted to talk about his ability, and Dorran hadn't pushed.

He had more than enough problems of his own right now. He didn't need to add yet another one.

He put the box in the guest room. Eli could take care of unpacking and finding places for stuff later. When Dorran turned to go back to the living room, he found it full of people.

Eli's family had arrived.

They brought the last boxes with them, and Dorran stepped to the side so they could take them to the guest room. The room was full, and he wasn't sure how he'd manage to get to his computer to work, but it wasn't something he wanted to think about right now.

Right now, he wanted to relax. He wasn't sure it was something he could do, though. This was the first time he had Eli's family over for lunch, and he was nervous. Why had he thought baking a lasagna was a good idea? It was something Eli's mother cooked often, and there was no way people wouldn't compare the two. What if Dorran's wasn't as good? Or what if it was better and she got offended?

"You look like you're about to bolt," Francis murmured.

Dorran could see Mel peeking at Francis every so often, but

he ignored Francis. He didn't want Eli's family to think he was crazy. He was already having a hard enough time with them.

"You're early," he said when they turned to look at him.

Eli's father laughed. "We wanted to help."

"Oh, you don't have to. We're basically done. Eli has to do the next step and empty his boxes."

Eli's brother snorted. "What he meant was that he called Eli and made sure he was almost finished before herding us out of the house. He didn't actually want to help. He wanted to act like he wanted to help."

Eli's father flushed, and everyone laughed. Dorran looked at Eli's mother, who was looking around, peering at everything. Dorran knew she was judging, seeing if this was a good enough place for her baby boy. He would have bristled at that once, but he understood she was doing it for love, not because she hated him. She didn't, even though she might not exactly love him.

She turned and caught Dorran's gaze. Dorran held his breath, wondering what was about to happen. Would she have something to say about the apartment? Or about the neighborhood? And if there was something she didn't like, would she say it out loud in front of everyone, or would she wait until she could get Eli alone and complain to him?

She smiled. "I like this place. It's really you, Dorran."

Dorran released the breath. "Thank you."

Dorran jumped when Eli slid an arm around his waist, then relaxed and leaned against him. "It's great, isn't it?"

This was Dorran's life now. Sunday lunches, lasagnas, and everything else.

Hopefully, it wouldn't be ruined by a new murder.

You may also enjoy the following from eXtasy Books Inc:

Fire and Earth
Catherine Lievens

Excerpt

Dakota didn't like this. He already knew everything there was to know about this case, but he always liked to listen to the people involved explain it. He also enjoyed Benedict's voice, but that didn't change the situation.

Someone was threatening Benedict, and it wouldn't end well if Dakota didn't put an end to it.

"They did. I got the first letter a few weeks after the attempted kidnapping. I'd already signed the deal by then, but I have several more in the works."

"Do you have the letters?" Most people would have thrown them away, so Dakota didn't expect much of this. He was surprised when managing nodded.

"I kept them. I wasn't sure they were serious in the beginning, but I didn't want to risk it. They're in my safe."

"I'll want to see them."

"Of course. We can go get them as soon as we're done with the conversation."

Dakota nodded. "Go on."

"I don't remember the precise days in which I got the others, except, of course, for the last one. I got that one yesterday."

"How are they delivered to you? Do they pass through the post?"

"I didn't check. I should have, but my secretary always gives me the mail, and I didn't think to check."

"Were the letters in envelopes?"

"They were."

"As long as you kept them, we can check if they were and delivered to your secretary or not. Can you tell me what the letters say?"

Benedict shrugged one shoulder. "The usual, I suppose. Not that I've ever received threatening letters before, of course. But it's obvious they want me to stop making business deals with other elements. Yesterday's letter told me to stop unless I want someone to get hurt, though. They're becoming shorter and more to the point."

That wasn't good. Most people would probably think in men's whoever was behind the letters was losing interest, but Dakota knew better. They'd warned Benedict several times, but he wasn't listening. It wouldn't be long before they attacked him instead of sending him letters.

Quillan had done the right thing calling Dakota.

"And you have no idea who's behind it?" Dakota asked.

"They were never signed. I suppose they're the same people who tried to kidnap Rhea, but that's all I know about it."

Dakota tapped his fingertips onto the marble counter. "I've already asked my people to look into it. Several groups don't like the mixing of elements, but we haven't been able to pinpoint which one is doing this yet."

"Yet? I have to say I'm impressed you're already looking into it."

"We started yesterday as soon as Quillan called me to let me know what was going on." Dakota straightened. "I need you to understand something. I know you insisted on paying my men and me, and that's okay. I won't protest because they deserve to be paid for the work they do. But that's not the reason I'm doing this. You're Rhea's father, and Rhea is Quillan's mate. That makes all of us family as far as I'm concerned, and that is the main reason I agreed to take this job."

Benedict wrinkled his nose, and it shouldn't have been as adorable as it was.

And Dakota shouldn't be thinking about how adorable Benedict was.

This was a job and a serious one at that. Dakota needed to be a hundred percent in the game. He couldn't allow himself to lose focus, no matter how hot Benedict was.

And he definitely was.

Dakota usually dated people closer to his age, but Benedict was a silver fox. Dakota could see where Rhea had gotten his looks from, and he couldn't deny he was attracted to Benedict. He would have to take himself off the job if things escalated, but he hoped they wouldn't. He cared about this. He needed to keep Benedict, Rhea, and Quillan safe, and that was what he'd do. If there could be anything between him and Benedict, it would have to happen later, once the case was over and everyone was safe.

"Is there anything else we can do?" Benedict asked.

"Well, as I said, we're already looking into several groups who might be behind this. Until we have more information, though, I don't think so."

"You're going to assign my father a bodyguard?" Rhea asked. "Because he needs one. He was going to work on his own this morning, and I don't think that's a good idea. He's only received letters so far, but I doubt whoever is behind this is going to stop here. They won't, and I'm afraid that the next step will be hurting my father. That can't happen."

"I agree," Dakota said.

Rhea blinked. "You do?"

"I do. You're right. I don't know if the same group was behind your attempted kidnapping and the letters, but if they are, I find it weird that they de-escalated rather than the other way around. The letters will last for much longer. It's obvious they're not working, and these people want something to happen. If your father doesn't listen to them, they'll take the next step and make sure he can't continue doing this."

"I don't want people following me around," Benedict stopped. "They'll think I'm afraid of them. They'll think the letters are working, and they're not. I'm not backing down. I want Quillan and Rhea to be safe, but I won't accept a body-guard."

Rhea threw his hands in the air. "You won't accept a bod-yguard? Are you crazy? I was almost kidnapped, and the same could happen to you, or worse. Do you want me to be an orphan?"

Dakota didn't have a say in this. He could suggest Benedict needed to have a bodyguard follow around, but he couldn't force his client to accept. It would be stupid not to, but it wasn't Dakota's place to say it.

On the other hand, it was precisely Rhea's place to do it.

"Of course I don't," Benedict said, raking a hand through his perfectly styled hair, messing them up. It made him look more human, and even more gorgeous, which shouldn't have been possible. "But I don't want these people to think I'm afraid of them."

"Maybe you should be. They're threatening you. They could kill you. I won't allow you to put your life in danger this way. We called Dakota for a reason, and you're going to listen to him."

Benedict glared at Rhea. "You do realize I am your father, not the other way around, right?"

"I do, and I don't care."

Quillan cleared his throat. "Benedict, is the only reason you don't want a bodyguard that the people who wrote the letters might think you're afraid of them?"

"Yes. I understand I need to be protected. I might not like it, but I don't want Rhea to be an orphan, as he unhelpfully pointed out."

"So we need a bodyguard who doesn't look like one."

Benedict rolled his eyes. "How is that supposed to happen?"

Quillan looked at Dakota, and Dakota knew he wouldn't like what was about to come out of his friend's mouth from his expression. "Dakota doesn't often take bodyguard jobs, but he used to do it in the beginning, and I'm sure he still can. You can tell people he's your boyfriend."

Dakota had been right. He didn't like this.

"What are you talking about?" Benedict asked.

Rhea snickered. "He can be your boy-toy. With the age difference, people won't suspect it's not the truth. As long as you can act like you're smitten with him, it shouldn't be a problem."

"I can't lie to people. Besides, who is going to believe Dakota is my boyfriend?"

"Who wouldn't?"

"He's half my age."

Dakota might not be happy about the suggestion, but he couldn't deny it had merit. Besides, he was amused by Benedict's outrage over it. "Not half your age," he drawled. He knew Benedict was forty-seven. "It's flattering, but I'm thirty-five. I suppose you could be my father if you'd started having sex early, though."

"What are you talking about? This isn't possible," Benedict said.

Dakota shrugged. "I'm game if you are. I can't deny it's a good idea. It would give me a reason to stick around, especially if we go with the boy-toy thing. People might be concerned, and they will no doubt ask questions, but like Quillan said, as long as you can fake being in love with me, people would probably believe it. No one knows about the letters except us, right?"

"I didn't tell anyone else."

"So like I said, they'll probably wonder what's happening,

but they won't say anything. You're their boss."

And he was Dakota's, too. This was going to complicate everything.

ABOUT THE AUTHOR

Catherine lives in Italy, country of good food and hot men. She used to write fantasy as a child, but it was reading her first gay erotic romance novel that made her realize that that was what she really wanted to write.

After graduating from college in English language and translation, she divides her day between writing, reading, taking care of her son and reading some more.

You can find her on Facebook and Twitter or on her website: authorcatherinelievens.wordpress.com

Email: lievens.catherine@gmail.com

Newsletter: http://eepurl.com/c-uvKn

Bookbub: https://www.bookbub.com/authors/catherine-lievens